THE GIRL WITH NO LAST NAME

DAVID CHILCOTT

ALSO BY DAVID CHILCOTT:

Murphy's Heist
Cruise The Storm
Find My Brother
The Ponzi Men
Trouble in Chicago
The Girl with No Last Name

First Edition

Copyright © 2018 David Chilcott
All rights reserved.
ISBN: 9781726797627

All rights reserved. No part of this book may be reproduced or transmitted in any form or by any means, electronic or mechanical, including photocopying, recording, or any information storage and retrieval system without prior written permission of the author.

The following is a work of fiction. Any resemblance to persons living or dead is purely coincidental, or used in the form of parody.

CHAPTER 1

The girl walked up to John McBride. She was extremely thin and dressed in 1950's clothes, aged about mid to late twenties. She opened her small handbag, pulled out a handkerchief, wiped her mouth, and put it back. Her right hand palmed a small square of paper, and she snapped the bag shut.

"Mr. McBride?" She could hardly be mistaken; McBride's face was on the huge posters in the entrance to the art gallery. McBride smiled at her.

She said, "May I congratulate you on a great show. Your paintings are all just so wonderful. However, we must be going now." She held out her right hand, and McBride grasped it and shook it. The piece of paper was in her hand, so McBride put his thumb over it. He could tell by her face that he had done what she wanted: to take the paper without anyone else being aware. Like maybe she didn't want the older couple who were with her, just a couple of feet behind also dressed in 1950's clothing, to know.

"What have you just given to the man?"

"Nothing." The girl turned round to face the couple. McBride, when he was a child of about twelve had an ambition to be a magician when he grew up. This was the time of television magic shows. For two years he had spent all his spare time practicing sleight of hand. It paid off now. McBride spread his hands out palms upwards, and then reversed them to show the backs. Nothing. Then as he brought his arms down, his right hand brushed his pocket and the paper square dropped in unnoticed.

The man, who wore a trilby hat perched on his head, and starched collar on his shirt said, "I'm sorry, I thought you gave the man something, I was mistaken." They all turned and walked towards the exit. McBride stood and watched them go.

Last night had been the preview of McBride's show which would run for three weeks in Sydney. After that there were shows in Melbourne and Perth. The previous three weeks McBride had painted day and night to record much of Sydney and its environs. So he would take it easy over the show period, attending the show only sporadically. On the last day he was committed to do a demonstration painting, which would be auctioned off for charity.

At twelve noon McBride's agent, Ian Smith, breezed in, looking left and right, judging the popularity of the exhibition by the number of people attending. He nodded and spoke to McBride.

"I'm just going to have lunch, do you want to eat with me?"

McBride never turned down Smith's offers. They came rarely enough. They both walked down the street to a small bistro fronting the road. A row of tables with red tablecloths, white parasols above each table made an attractive frontage.

Smith pushed open the glass door, said, "I couldn't get an outside table, they were booked solid."

"It doesn't matter, there's a breeze, the napkins will probably blow away. And I might be pestered by people demanding autographs."

"You wish."

The Maître d' bustled over, actually bowed, and led them to a corner table. He opened the napkins, placed them over their knees when they were seated, handed them a menu each, and rushed away again.

McBride reached into his pocket, pulled out the square of paper, opened it out and smoothed it against the table cloth. It was approximately A5 size, a fly leaf from a paperback it looked like, one edge with tear marks where it had been removed from a book. One side had a printed verse on it, the other side contained hand writing in blue biro.

Smith saw what he was doing. "Fan mail are you getting now?"

"A girl who had come to the gallery with an older couple, gave it to me. Maybe it's fan mail. I'm trying to work out what the subject is."

"For goodness sake. Don't get tied up in some more dangerous situations, like you did in the States."

"That wasn't my fault. I sometimes think that trouble seeks me out." McBride started reading the note.

"That's what I told you. It does."

McBride didn't reply, but carried on reading.

Help me. I am confined in a cult as a prisoner. I have just stolen a cell phone and I will switch it on every night from nine o'clock to 10 o'clock, Tuesday to Thursdays inclusive. Please phone and I will tell you more."

Underneath was printed the telephone number. McBride handed the note to Smith just as the waiter arrived with his order pad. Smith looked up.

"I'll have a steak, sirloin, rare, a few chipped potatoes, broccoli, please."

The waiter turned to McBride, pencil poised. "Fish, please, the monkfish."

"And to drink?"

Smith said, "A good bottle of claret, please."

McBride said, "Just a glass of Chablis if you have it."

"Yes, Sir." And he went away.

Smith said, "This note is probably a foolish joke."

"There is that. But it might not be. The girl was very nervous, and very thin."

"What about the couple she was with?"

"Overbearing and terrifying to be with, it seemed."

"Still think you're the fall guy."

Smith stayed in the restaurant until he had finished his wine. The whole bottle. McBride stayed with him sipping coffee and people watching. He was in no hurry. He wouldn't go back to the gallery until the next day.

The message he had received that morning kept coming back to his mind. Today was Wednesday, he could phone her this evening.

Eventually Smith stood up, having already paid the bill. He pulled a few dollars from his pocket, left them by his wineglass. They walked out together.

They were only a short walk from their apartment, a reason for choosing it, so that they could easily get to the gallery. McBride, as an artist, was constantly looking at the views around him while he walked, weighing up what would make a good watercolor. In Sydney all the views were overpowering. Smith appeared deep in thought.

He spoke as they walked up an incline towards the apartment. "You are going to phone the girl who gave you the note?"

"Maybe. I haven't made a final decision. Yes, probably."

"You could pass it to the police."

"I don't know whether they bother about cults. You don't hear about them raiding such places."

"There was the big raid on the Manson people wasn't there?"

"I wasn't even born, I think." He glanced at Smith, gave him a cheeky smile.

Smith looked back at McBride. "It was in America, that's all I can remember. I was very young." He grinned back at McBride.

Chapter 2

McBride spent the evening indoors the following day. It was Wednesday, one of the specified nights that he could phone the girl from the cult. He had tried several times the previous night. But every time he rang, the message was *sorry, this number is not available. Please leave a message.* He didn't leave a message and came to the conclusion she may still be in Sydney, or traveling home, wherever that was. At least it was a genuine number that she had written down.

When he and Smith got home from eating out, he sat down in the lounge and read the morning paper again. It was as boring as the first time. At nine o'clock Smith said he was going to bed to watch television.

McBride watched the clock, being patient enough not to pick up the phone until ten past the hour. Then he dialed the number which he now knew from memory.

It rang out for several seconds, and then a breathless voice spoke quietly.

"Hello."

This is John McBride. You invited me to phone. I tried you last night, but got no reply."

"We didn't get back from Sydney until eleven o'clock. Sorry."

"Nothing to be sorry for. What is your name?"

"Lucy. I don't have a last name."

"That is strange. Most people have a last name."

"I don't."

"How are you?"

"Hungry!"

"Why are you so thin? Don't you get enough to eat?"

"If I want food, I have to do things I would rather not."

McBride thought he ought to change the subject.

"Where do you live? Is it near Sydney?"

"About four hours' drive. It is near Dulong."

"How long have you been with the cult?"

"I don't know. I had only just learned to walk when I came."

"When I saw you, you were with two older people. Were they your mother and father?" The age gap would have been about right.

"No. They are my guiding angels. That is what they say. I have lived with them since I came to the place they call the Children of Messiah. I must go now. Will you telephone me again? Please."

McBride always considered himself a hard man, being an ex SAS soldier. But the way she said *please* brought tears to his eyes. For a long time after the call had ended he sat in the chair going over the conversation in his mind.

***

The next day McBride decided to talk to the Sydney Police. He looked online and saw the address of the Australian Federal Police. It sounded as good a start as any.

It wasn't too far, so he walked. It was a large building on a junction of two streets. Inside the main lobby was a reception desk.

"I want to speak to someone about a cult situated near Sydney."

"A what, Sir?" She was a fortyish woman, trim and maybe even a policewoman rather than a civilian.

McBride tried again. "I met someone a few days ago who belonged to a cult, an organization. I got the impression she was being held against her will."

"I'll see if I can get someone to interview you. If you will just sit over there." She pointed to a row of seats across against the wall. He went over and sat down on a chair next to a bearded man who didn't look as though he had washed for a long time. The seat next to him was the only empty one. He realized why when he sat down. He smelled as though he hadn't washed for a long time as well. McBride sat there for twenty minutes by his watch, and was just thinking about going back to the desk when a smartly dressed man in a sports jacket with a clipboard in his hand crossed the lobby to the seating. He was maybe about McBride's age, early forties, trim, not overweight.

"Mr. McBride," he called, glancing at the clipboard. McBride stood up. "Will you come this way, Sir." The man turned on his heel, and went down a corridor without waiting to see if McBride followed. At a door set into the left hand wall, he paused to slide a notice from the door which said *vacant*, turn the notice over and push it back in its groove. The notice now read *occupied.*

The man pushed his way into the room, flicking on the light switch as he did so. He stood back to allow McBride into the room ahead of him, and let the door close. The space was about ten feet square, with a metal desk and two chairs. The man sat down at the desk, and indicated that McBride take the other chair.

"Mr. McBride, I'm Sergeant Hopkins, Jack Hopkins." He pulled a ballpoint pen out of his pocket, put the clipboard on the desk, leaned back and looked at McBride. "You want to tell me why you're here? Something about a kidnap?"

"Not exactly that. Let me start at the beginning. I came from England to exhibit my watercolors at certain galleries, one of which is here in Sydney. A couple of days ago, while I was in the gallery a girl in her twenties approached me. She knew I was the artist. She stood in front of me, and opened her purse under the pretense of getting her handkerchief out. I saw that she had palmed a small folded piece of paper. It was obvious that what she wanted me to see it. When she shook my hand she was pleased that I palmed the paper. She was with two older people, a couple. The man was angry, he was sure that she was passing me a note. Then he apologized, and they left.

"She had left her phone number, a cell number, and asked me to phone her at a certain time."

The policeman smiled. "You pulled there. What are you complaining about?"

"If you had been there, you wouldn't have thought that. She was painfully thin, and, well, she seemed helpless. Anyway I phoned her as she had asked, and she gave me a bit more information. First she told me she was always hungry. She said she had to do things that she didn't want to do, to be given food. She told me the name of the cult. It is called the Children of Messiah, near Dulong. Have you any information on it? Is it known to the police?"

He took a plastic card from his pocket, put it into a slot in the computer keyboard. The screen powered up, and the sergeant entered the name the Children of Messiah. After a second or two, script came up on the screen.

He was quiet for a moment while he read it. Then he said, "Nothing bad. Just a note that a cult called Children of Messiah is located on the road out of Dulong, membership estimated at twenty to thirty people living in one building, with some farming activity. So they've never committed any crime we've heard of."

"That doesn't mean they aren't bad. Just circumspect."

"Yes, indeed. Are you here to lodge a complaint?

"Not at the moment. Are there a lot of Cults in Australia? I mean, America seems full of them."

"If we've got a lot of cults, they don't make waves. After all, a cult isn't dangerous in itself."

McBride said, "I would beg to differ. The biggest cult in the western world nearly wiped out civilization."

"Never heard of that one. What was it called?"

"The Nazis. A typical cult. One man running the organization surrounded by sycophants carrying out his orders. Adolf Hitler."

The sergeant smiled. "Caught me out there. Should we be bombing the Children of Messiah?"

"Bit early for that. Wouldn't harm to keep it watched."

"If you come up with any further evidence naturally you can be sure we'll listen to you. And I'll make a note of this discussion." He stood up, the meeting at an end.

When McBride got back to the apartment, Ian Smith, his agent, was up and dressed, sitting in an easy chair drinking tea. Goodness, thought McBride, he had run out of wine again.

"Where did you go? I thought you might have been down at the gallery, but when I rang they said you hadn't visited since yesterday morning."

"I went to the police station. To report that Messiah cult the girl belonged to."

"And the police are going to raid it?"

"No. They aren't going to do anything."

"This afternoon I fly over to Melbourne, to fix up the next exhibition, and after that straight on to Perth. Same again. Then back to England. I won't see you until you get to Perth. I've got a lot of work to do back home."

"I'm going to hire a car and drive to Dulong and investigate the cult. If the police won't do it, then I'll have to. Give my love to Blighty, and phone occasionally to see how the exhibition's doing."

CHAPTER 3

McBride went out to hire a car that afternoon, although he would not set out for Dulong until early the following morning. When the cab dropped him off at the depot, McBride was pleased to see mainly Toyota cars outside on the forecourt.

There was a young man on the reception inside, who smiled pleasantly at McBride.

"What can I do for you today?" he enquired.

"I need to hire a car for a couple of days. Perhaps a Toyota Auris hybrid, if you have one."

"Sure, Sir, that's no problem." McBride, although he had not long been in Australia, was becoming used to the locals having no problem with anything, apparently.

"Perhaps you'll have a map as well. I'm intending on going to Dulong."

"Yessir." He reached under the counter, laid an A4 printed sheet on the countertop. "That's along the Great Western Highway. You go through the Blue Mountains once you're out of Sydney. They're part of the Great Divide range. Take care how you drive through the mountains. The road is narrow with lots of bends. It's built on the original explorers' route. Once you get through the hills onto the plain, look for a right on to the Castlereagh Highway. It's hard to miss. It leads right through Dulong." He also began to explain the route out of the city itself which took some doing apparently.

McBride drove back to his apartment with the impression that he was about to undertake a hazardous expedition. Then he remembered the girl's angels who had made it back home in darkness.

He set off early the next morning, just before seven, and beat most of the rush hour traffic. He was surprised to see how quickly the ground began to rise almost as soon as he cleared the last of the suburbs. The sky was blue, a cloudless day. The clerk at the car hire depot had warned that there was often fog in the mountains. Not today, though. He drove with the driver's window down and the smell of the eucalyptus trees was overpowering. As predicted, the curves were tight, the road clinging to cliff walls as it followed the gorges that abounded. But the mountains weren't high, just big hills. It was slow going though, following large trucks with no hope of overtaking.

As he entered the last curving downhill stretch of the mountains he could see a vast grassy plain stretching for miles ahead of him, dotted with bushes and straggly trees. There were cattle in abundance, and occasional farm buildings. It looked like England of the 1950s. He could almost be going back in time. He remembered the 1950's dress of the Children of Messiah. Weird.

He didn't miss turning on to the Castlereagh Highway. It would have been hard to miss, as the clerk at the depot had told him. The road was even quieter than the road through the mountains. Occasionally he passed through small villages, hamlets really mostly built in conjunction with farms and agricultural needs. There was another range of hills far in the distance, just a smudge on the horizon. The day was still sunny, green grass of the verges studded with buttercups, rabbits making kamikaze dashes across the road occasionally. The journey took just the predicted four hours, and he was entering Dulong. It wasn't big, that was immediately apparent. The main street, called Main Street was mostly single storey buildings, looking like a western cowboy town in the United States. The street was wide meaning cars could be parked diagonally to the curb. There were plenty of parking spaces here today at nearly lunchtime. Near enough to make McBride declare it was *his* lunch time. He parked and got out of his car, stretching himself from the long drive, looking around for a café. He saw the Bakers Coffee Shop, and made a beeline for it. The menu in the window told him it was mostly pies: beef, mutton, rabbit. Well, why not? He went in regardless. He was hungry and had a very substantial lunch.

When he came out in the street after eating he noticed way further on there was a filling station, two lonely pumps on a large open concrete forecourt. McBride thought that by topping the tank up he could get some free information on the location of the cult. He got back in his car and drove the short distance to the garage. As he approached the pump labeled lead-free petrol an old man in dark blue overalls came out of the corrugated iron workshop to attend to him.

McBride jumped out of the car, and said, "Fill it up, please." The old man pulled a lever down on the side of the pump, and then put the nozzle into the car. He spat into a fire bucket ten feet away by the diesel pump. He hit the bucket without touching the sides. Tobacco juice. McBride noticed the brown stained teeth, and the wedge tucked into his cheek. The man wiped his mouth with the back of his overall sleeve. A dark streak in the cloth showed it had been done often before. He needed a shave, his chin bristled silver in the sunlight.

The old man clicked off the pump, hung up the pipe and fastened the petrol cap on the car. McBride reached in his pocket pulled out some dollars waiting for the man to give him the price.

"That'll be... let's see," he scratched his head, screwed up his eyes, and said, "say ten dollars, that's rounding it down." It seemed very cheap for the distance he had driven. When he looked at the pump register, he saw that it was broken, still registering zero dollars. Shrugging, McBride counted out ten dollars, gave the notes to the man, and added an extra note. "That's the tip," he said.

"Why, thank you, first tip I've had in what, ten years?"

"Can I just ask you to tell me something? There's a sort of cult somewhere near here, called the Children of Messiah. Have you heard of it?"

The old guy grinned, laughed to himself for a minute. "Of course. The guy who started it up – why I went to school with him. He was in the same class. Not a nice boy, allus after the little girls, pulling their drawers down. When the teachers caught him they used to cane him something horrid. Never did stop him doing dirty things. After he left school, he was waiting around the town, ready to rape any woman who was alone. All the women they learned to go around in company, never by themselves." He paused, and thought. "At first they used to put him in the town jail. In the end they put him in the county jail for three years I think it was. He went away after that."

He spat expertly across to the fire bucket, and wiped his mouth on his sleeve.

"Then he came back years later, bought up some land and built a wooden hut on it. 'bout fifty acres. Then he put a sign up by the roadside "Children of Messiah". He had a few guys with him, then some women came, and they started collecting young girls, never boys. The folk, they rarely go out. The place is guarded by men with rifles. I wouldn't go there, if I were you."

McBride stared at him. "My God," he said. "That means there is at least one pedophile in that shack, maybe more. Do the police know?"

"Shouldn't think so. Do you know what the population of this town is? Two thousand or thereabouts. And we have a police station. Not a very big one, naturally, and not always open. Staff of one policeman and one woman civilian to look after the front desk."

McBride climbed into his car, and drove out of the forecourt, in the direction the old man had pointed. He drove slowly, enjoying the afternoon sun. The road was rising slowly, when he reached the crest, he saw it. A long wooden building about fifty feet back off the road, gable end towards the road, so the building stretched back, maybe one hundred and fifty feet long, and thirty feet deep. It was behind a tall steel fence about ten or twelve feet tall, gaps between the vertical rods maybe six or eight inches. At the base chicken wire reached up a couple of feet to keep the rabbits out. The steel fence itself would keep the 'roos out, too.

He pulled up off the road where an earth track spread with hardcore ran parallel along the building. He pulled a map out of the glove box, got out of the car, and spread the map on the roof, pretended to study it. He waited for reaction from the building.

It came quickly. After about five minutes McBride saw a gate in the fence open, and a man in overalls stepped out. He was carrying a rifle butt down in his right hand. He headed up the track towards the car. McBride looked up from the map, still holding it down as it flapped in the breeze. As the guy got closer, McBride could identify the rifle as an old Lee Enfield. It had to be old, because the British army, the last to use the rifle, had ditched them in the early sixties. It used .303 ammunition, and was accurate to four hundred yards, if it had the optional scope sight. The design dated to 1900, over a hundred years ago, but it was still a good weapon. But why had he chosen it? Too powerful to shoot rabbits, that was for sure. The man was tanned and now he was nearer he could see that he was fiftyish, and in good trim.

"Good afternoon," said McBride.

"This here's private land."

"I never thought anything else, but I'm parked on the roadside. And this side of your name sign." Children of Messiah on a small post at the side of the track.

"Well, we don't admit visitors. We just keep ourselves to ourselves. I would advise you to move along." He hefted the rifle.

McBride folded the map and climbed back in the car, drove off. He didn't need a bullet in his face, or anywhere else. He looked over at the Children of Messiah as he drove along. A balcony ran all the way along the building, with eaves extending over. The front and back of the building within the fence was an extensive vegetable garden. Alongside the plot was a large field with a barn and sheep and cattle. Away behind the building McBride could see a windmill maybe driving a water pump. In the vegetable gardens he could see young women not unlike Lucy, hoeing and picking. They seemed to be wearing blue dungarees. Some kind of uniform, maybe. Or maybe gardening rig only.

He turned round a mile or two later and drove slowly back into town, He wasn't ready to return to Sydney tonight, there was more he needed to learn.

Back in Dulong, the town was drowsing in the sun, barely any pedestrians. He saw a sign pointing to the police station, followed it and saw a bungalow part residential, part office. A post in the garden bore the single word: POLICE.

Chapter 4

McBride went up the garden path, opened the door, and a bell jangled. He went into a small front room furnished merely with a metal desk and a metal filing cabinet. In a chair behind the desk, a woman of about thirty-five in a flowered dress sat doing her nails.

"Oh, you gave me a fright," she said. She put the nail file down. "Can I help you?"

"Is the police man in?" Without standing up, she swung the chair round and pulled open the door behind her. "Are you there, Stan?"

After a moment a large man of about fifty in shirt sleeves and uniform trousers, came into the outer office.

The woman gestured to McBride. "This gentleman wants to see you. I'm sorry, Sir, I didn't get your name."

"John McBride. I really need to talk to you about the Children of Messiah."

The policeman looked at McBride for a few seconds without saying anything, then said, "Come through into my office." McBride squeezed past the woman's desk and through the door. The policeman's office was as small as the front office, with a replica metal desk and two chairs. Spread out on the desk was a daily newspaper, open at the racing pages. Caught in the act, McBride smiled inwardly.

"My name is Sergeant Stan Burrows, sit down." The sergeant sat down, folded up the paper, and put it on the floor. "I've got quite a lot on, but tell me why you need to talk." A lot on, like phoning up the bookie perhaps?

"I met a member of the Children of Messiah, in Sydney, actually. She was a young lady in her twenties, and looked very under-nourished. I drove over here, but when I got to the church, home or whatever you call it, a man appeared with a rifle in his hand, and was quite abusive."

"What do you want me to do?" the sergeant said. "Firstly it is a private organization, been here many years, and never cause any trouble. Was the gun loaded?"

"It was an old Lee Enfield, you don't answer the door with a rifle of that caliber in your hands."

"It likely wasn't loaded. He didn't shoot at you did he?"

"He might have done if I hadn't beat it fast."

He stood up. "Well, no harm done."

McBride said, "Well you haven't heard everything yet." He continued to sit.

The sergeant sat down again with obvious reluctance. "Carry on," he said.

"Before I went to the cult, sect, or whatever you call it, I filled up with petrol down the road, spoke with the old fellow. He seemed to have a few things to tell about them."

The sergeant winced. "He's not exactly a nutter, but he does guess what you owe him, instead of getting the pump fixed. I suppose he told you about Harold Fox, eh?"

"If that is what the founder of the Children of Messiah is called, then yes. He said the guy was put away on a rape charge."

The policeman nodded, as though pleased at catching someone out. "But he didn't tell you that he doesn't run the cult no more? Hasn't done since he caught the cancer. Luckily he's cured now, so I hear. Lives in a big house back of the main street."

"Then you've put my mind at rest," said McBride, and stood up. "What do they call the reverend gentleman?"

"The reverend gentleman? Who you talking about?"

I thought you said someone else was in charge of the Children of Messiah? I just assumed it would be a churchman."

"Oh. He's called Pepper. Could be a reverend. Looks like one. I seem to mind he wears a dog collar."

McBride stood on the police station doorstep and looked at his watch. Still only two o'clock. He didn't feel like staying overnight in this one horse town. He had a lot to think about, but he could do that back in Sydney, and he ought to attend the gallery tomorrow. Time to be on the road. Four hours, he would easily be back before dark.

He made better time than he thought he would. He knew the way, and he made it in three and a half hours to his apartment. As he walked in the door, he saw the *Sydney Daily Herald* on the floor, and picked it up. It gave him an idea.

In the sitting room he used the phone and made a call. The *Daily Herald* phone was picked on the third ring. He asked for the news room.

"Jim Hoskin here, the Newsroom are busy just now. Can I help you?"

"It's possible. This is John McBride speaking. I'm over in Sydney from England and…"

Hoskins cut in "You're the watercolor artist aren't you? Could I fix up to interview you? I'm the art critic on the paper. Sorry, carry on…"

"Well the answer to your query is that I would be pleased for you to interview me. The reason I phoned is whether you have any information on a cult called the Children of Messiah. I met a member when I was in the gallery. She worried me. In fact I went over to Dulong today. I didn't get in to the cult premises. A man came out with a gun and threatened to shoot me."

"Tell you what I can look through the files, we've got a really up-to-date system, it will spew any information out and I'll let you have it. Are you free tonight I leave in half an hour, I could treat you to dinner. What do you say?"

"I say that you are an impulsive person, and yes you can buy me dinner. When and where?"

They agreed to meet at seven at the Guillotine.

***

McBride walked into the bar of the Guillotine and there was only one person, a youngish man sitting there.

"Mr. Hoskin?" The man stood up off the seat by the bar counter. About thirty years old, slender, tanned face under a shock of fair hair. Your typical Aussie.

"John McBride? I'm very pleased to meet you. Let me buy you a drink."

McBride knew they were going to get on well. The youngster oozed bon-homie, he genuinely seemed to be enjoying himself.

"Just a half of lager please." The barman was waiting for the order hand poised over the pumps. The foaming beer was dispensed in seconds.

"Hey, before I forget," said Hoskin, plunging his hand inside his jacket, and withdrawing a bundle of paper. "There's all that we have on your cult."

"I'm surprised you got all this on the subject. Thank you."

"Sure, it surprised me as well when all those pages chugged out of the printer. Haven't read them, though."

Hoskin conducted the interview over dinner, but he did it skillfully and it might have been just two friends conversing. Hoskin didn't take many notes. By the time they got to the dessert course he had wrapped the interview up, and they got to talking about Australia itself. The newspaperman was a native of Sydney, and it had been his job since college. He admitted that a job in the news room was his ambition.

They parted at the door of the restaurant. It was dark, and McBride was tired. Today already he had driven for nearly eight hours, talked to the police, and the newspaperman. They waved to each other, vowing to meet again.

When McBride got into his apartment he was yawning, and didn't even look at the printouts that young Hoskin had given him, but left them on the sitting room table and went to bed.

CHAPTER 5

Next morning McBride was up early. After a breakfast of rye toast and an apple, he took his coffee into the sitting room. He picked up the *Herald's* printouts and sat down to read them.

He realized at once that the articles were in date order, starting with the oldest. It was headlined *New Cult started in Dulong.*

'June 1973. Harold Fox, the Dulong resident given a three-year sentence for rape, has been released and is back in Dulong setting up a cult called Children of Messiah. It will be based in a wooden house built on a 50 acre plot just outside the town. Work is still continuing on the building and it is not thought that the cult is active yet.'

A month later another article headlined *Dulong cult opens for business.*

'We understand that the new cult Children of Messiah in Dulong is open for business. An opening ceremony was carried out by Harold Fox. There are several meeting rooms and lounges as well as single bedrooms. At one end of the building is a non-denominational church. Several people appear to be in residence, mainly young females.'

Nothing more was published until October 2002: *Cult leader ill*

Leader of the cult Children of Messiah is believed to be in hospital undergoing radiotherapy.

The last report was dated November 2002: *New Cult leader appointed in Dulong.*

'Harold Fox, the founder of Children of Messiah Cult appointed a minister to take charge of the cult. His name is Christopher Pepper, previously a member of the Mormon Church. Mr. Fox said, "I have every confidence in Pastor Pepper, who is a devout churchman." Mr. Fox is reputed to have been cured of his cancer, said to be prostate cancer, but will take no further part in the running of the cult, although he is believed to own the land and buildings.'

Typical filler material thought McBride. It didn't tell him a lot more than he already knew. He needed to go along there one night under cover of darkness and do a recce. But not yet, he needed to visit his exhibition, speak to customers, fulfill his obligations.

He spent the rest of the day at the gallery. The attendances were above the levels when the exhibition had first opened. The proprietor told McBride that good reviews in the press and even on television had worked well. Their publicity people also told them that word of mouth was contributing to the popularity of the exhibition, which was the best one that they had held for some years. At the behest of the gallery owner, McBride gave a short speech, during which he mentioned that he would be doing a demonstration painting on the last day. This would be auctioned and part of the proceeds would be given to charity. All in all it was a very good day for McBride. He returned to his apartment after stopping off for dinner at a bistro. He remembered Lucy, and decided to give her a telephone call. He looked in his wallet for the number and dialed it. After a short pause he got a recorded message: *You have dialed an incorrect number. Please check and dial again.* McBride did so, but with a sinking feeling that the number would never be answered. Somebody at the cult had found Lucy's phone.

The news made him determined to bring forward his next visit to Dulong.

He had meant to go during the early part of next week, but tomorrow was Friday. He could set off in the afternoon, spending the morning at the gallery, arriving as it was getting dark in Dulong.

It was six in the evening when McBride drove into Dulong. He drove towards Dulong's sole petrol station, hoping it was still open. He needed to speak to the old man again. He was pleased to see that there were a couple of lights showing over the pumps. He pulled in at the petrol pump, and tooted his horn. The shed door opened and the old man walked over to the pump. When he saw McBride, he smiled, recognizing him.

"Hello, Sir. Fill it up?"

"Yes please." McBride got out of the car and walked down the car to stand with the old man.

"You didn't tell me that Harold Fox wasn't running the cult these days."

"We didn't get that far through the story if you'll recall. Only up to the part where he started the cult and built the place." The pump clicked off, and the old man withdrew the nozzle, expertly inverting it to avoid spilling drips on the car's paintwork. McBride looked at the pump. Still not registering a price.

"Ten dollars, Sir,"

McBride proffered the money. "So the policeman I talked to said Harold Fox got cancer, was now cured, but lives in a big house in the village, and the cult has a priest who used to be a Mormon, called Pepper."

"You got that right, Sir." He turned to walk back to the shack.

"Wait a moment," McBride said, and the old man stopped, turned round to face him.

"Did Fox donate the buildings and land to the cult?"

The old man shook his head. "Of course not, old Fox needs an income to live in the style he does."

"So he rents the shed and the land to the cult? How can they afford to pay the rent? They don't get donations from anywhere do they?"

"Well in a manner of speaking, Sir."

"And?"

"Well I'm not one to go muck spreading, am I"

"You aren't?"

The old man shook his head and smiled. "Good night to you, Sir." And he disappeared into his corrugated metal shed, and closed the door behind him.

McBride got into his car. Before he started up the vehicle, he heard sounds of rumbling thunder away in the east. It was not going to be a good night for doing a recce.

McBride drove out of town for fifteen minutes, and slowed as he reached the long low building of the cult. Instead of stopping opposite the building on the verge of the road, he inched along slowly until he reached the limits of the site, just past the large field of sheep and cows. Whilst there were no turnouts here, there was a large verge with short grass without signs of hidden ruts or drainage channels. McBride pulled off the road and doused his lights. It was just twilight. To the east the sky was black with thunderclouds. Away to the west, the sky was bright with setting sun which had just disappeared below the far hills.

He got out of the car and locked the doors. He looked over the car roof at the land away from the cult property. It was grassland, with patches of barren earth and stones. But it would be possible to walk alongside the fence round the property, and he could see even in the failing light, scrubby trees and bushes behind the shed. That would be a good place to spy from. He had the field glasses in his pocket, and there should be nothing else he would need. If it rained, as it definitely looked as though it might, he would just get wet. That didn't kill you.

Chapter 6

It was tougher going than it looked. When McBride got alongside the fence heading west away from the road, he found nettle patches, up against the fence, so that he had to walk along away from them. As the sun dropped below the far mountain range, it was hard to see where he was stepping, and he tripped on large stones, and on one occasion got his foot caught in tumbleweed, and fell headlong to the ground. He picked himself up, and edged left, putting his left hand on the fence rail. He might get stung, but he would stay upright. He speeded up as a result, and got to the end of the fence in about half an hour. That meant the field was about a mile and a half long, or thereabouts.

The fence turned at ninety degrees to parallel the road, and he could see electric lights in the distance. He could also hear voices, conversation, men talking. He had thought that the cult had contained women only. Though why he had thought that he couldn't recall. Come to think now about it, he recalled the man accompanying Lucy at the gallery. That was one guy living here, and there must surely be other guarding angels of the male variety.

He walked a further mile and a half before the fence turned ninety degrees again. The long wooden building ended about two hundred yards away. In the space between he could see, in the electric lights attached to the rear wall, a car park with several saloon cars parked there, and pickups too. The voices had come from the men standing in groups, most of them drinking from the tinnies they clutched.

As he got nearer, he saw what they were waiting for. A door in the back of the building opened and the man who had accosted him with the rifle a week back, appeared and yelled a couple of names. A ragged cheer broke out and two men entered the building.

McBride didn't advance on the car park, but turned to the trees behind him, and was soon invisible from the car park. He stood under a largish tree, and scanned the crowd in front of the building. Crowd was a misnomer. He counted: seven cars and pickups, six men. Plus at least two inside the building. Twenty minutes later, the two men emerged from the doorway to loud cheers from the rest. They climbed into a pick-up, started it up, and roared up the track beside the building towards the road.

The clouds in front of McBride had advanced, and flashes of lightning were lighting the sky in an almost continuous light. He moved away from the tallest trees in the copse. Better to be safe than burned to a cinder. Thunder rumbled louder. He could hear raindrops hitting the leaves above him. The men were getting into their vehicles, but not driving off.

Five minutes later the storm reached the cult buildings. Thunder was nearly continuous, the sound blotting out the rush of wind through the trees, a wind that had arrived with the storm. A couple of cars moved out on the track and to the road. Given up waiting, guessed McBride. He was now certain this cult was being operated as a brothel. What a way to pay the rent that Harold Fox demanded! And even a way to pay a salary for Reverend Pepper?

As McBride was thinking about this he saw lightning hit the opposite end of the wooden building right on the apex of the roof, a huge explosion deafened him momentarily, and he saw flames lick along the roof. Clad with bitumen lightweight tiles rather than slate which would be too heavy for this cheaply built construction. The first of the tiles fell off the roof, setting the dry grass alight. Already the roof was a mass of flames, and McBride burst out of the copse and ran fast towards the building. On his way past the vehicles he bellowed for the men to help him. He climbed the steps at the end of the edifice, but the door was locked. He turned and raced to the double doors in the middle of the building, and he saw from the corner of his eye that one other man was on his heels.

They neared the door just as it opened and a girl in a nightdress staggered into the open air. McBride grabbed her by the arm.

"Where are the others? You should all be here outside, the building is burning down."

She looked at him, dazed. "They're all locked in their rooms. But my door doesn't lock properly, so I can get out."

McBride shook her. "Who has the keys?"

"Mr. Pepper."

"Where is he?"

"I don't know."

McBride gave up on her, remembered his cell phone, pulled it from his jacket, and dialed three zeros. "Fire and ambulance I'm speaking from the Children of Messiah Cult building near Dulong. The building is on fire and there are at least forty people trapped in the building. Yes, my name is John McBride."

Thrusting his phone in his pocket, he quickly followed the other man indoors. The entry corridor ended in a 'T' about a dozen feet in. He looked up and down the corridor. No sign of Pepper, or indeed anyone else except the man who had joined him from the car park. He was a well-built man, looked as if he might be a farm worker.

"Come on," McBride shouted. "Start here and go towards the fire, kicking down the doors like this."

He braced his back on the opposite wall and kicked violently out at the door on the other side. His shoe hit the door violently, just below the handle. The lock gave way and the door swung inward.

"Fire. Come out quickly. Get outside." A girl came sleepily out of the room.

The other man was mimicking McBride's actions on the doors at the opposite side of the corridor. McBride's hopes rose. He tackled the next door, then glanced in the direction of the fire. Smoke was rolling down the corridor. It was coming from the ceiling. Through the smoke which hung in a heavy pall from the ceiling to about three feet off the floor, he spotted a man lurching towards him. He was pausing to cough every couple of feet or so. He wore a dog collar. Certainly Reverend Pepper. He must have the keys. McBride rushed up the corridor towards the man, and caught him as he fell forward gasping. He shook him, but there was no reaction from the man. He was either unconscious, or feigning it. McBride plunged his hands through Pepper's pockets, searching for keys, after first feeling round his belt in case the keys were attached there. In his jacket pocket he found a large bunch of keys. He held them in front of his face, and riffled through them. He ignored the Yale type keys, McBride was searching for a mortise lock key.

McBride spotted a likely key, well-used and about the right size. He left Pepper on the floor, crawled to the next door that was locked, pushed the key in the aperture. It turned, and the door was unlocked. He wrenched the door open, hustled the girl out, and pushed her towards the exit.

"Hey, buster, I've got the keys. Pull the girls out as I open the doors." The farmworker turned and together they worked the corridor, freeing the women. And then the girls weren't walking out of their rooms unaided, they had to be dragged from their beds, and carried out semi-conscious. It took both McBride and the farm worker both carrying one girl between them. Outside, one of the girls released earlier took over and sat them on the grass. The work was going too slowly, they were losing the battle to the fire. And then McBride heard the fire engine sirens, coming louder as he listened. As he emerged from the building carrying another victim he saw the engine drive down the track, firemen dropping off the vehicle as it was still moving, fire hoses being unreeled. And the first splashes of water as the pumps surged into life. Four of the crew donned breathing apparatus, ready to go into the blazing building.

John McBride raced across to them. "You'll need this key, it unlocks all the bedrooms. The girls are locked in at night. There should be about forty altogether, including the ones we've already rescued." He swung an arm in the direction of the girls who were sitting, and in some cases lying on the grass of the track, well away from the blaze.

One of the firemen counted quickly. "That means there must be twenty-five at least still inside."

"And a few older ones, too."

The men pulled up their masks and ran into the building. Outside other firemen were on their way looking for a water supply. Their own tanks on the engines wouldn't hold much more water.

McBride pointed, and shouted. "There's a wind turbine over there. I think there's a well." He was pointing to the other side of the building. Another engine swept down the track as he spoke. More men appeared. Ambulances also arrived, two of them edging past the fire engines, on the grass edge of the track. McBride looked down at the rescued people, and the nurses heading towards them. He noticed Reverend Pepper sitting close by, and now recovered apparently. Undoubtedly he had heard McBride introduce himself to the fire crews. McBride was bad news to the cult, and Pepper undoubtedly knew this. He was eyeing McBride with distaste. *The feeling was mutual.*

That night's battle with the fire was long and difficult. The fire crew tried very hard to save the half of the building which was untouched when they arrived. It was a valiant attempt, but when the wind increased at about three in the morning the fire jumped the waterlogged roof and walls, and began burning the roof of the remaining building. At least by this time the building had been completely evacuated. This fight had not been in vain. Lives had been saved. The final total of deaths was thirteen. Ambulances had made many journeys to the hospital in Dulong, and also to the morgue. Of those that were hospitalized, three were in a critical condition.

As the fire brigade damped down the ashes, and the sun was rising over the mountains to the east, McBride was in conversation with the crew captain. They were both sitting on the ground against the boundary fence eyeing the smoking ruin, with the crew still using hoses on the stubborn flames. The air held a charcoal smell.

McBride was weary, his clothes charred, dirt smearing his face and hands. Both McBride and the crew captain held mugs of sweet tea, which they swigged at thirstily. McBride said, "Sid, I told you all the girls were locked in their bedrooms. That was the reason for the deaths as you will appreciate. I have another concern. I think the cult was running a brothel and that some of the girls were being forced into prostitution against their will. I think the money earned went in part to Harold Fox to pay the rent, and the rest to Pepper. What will you do with this information?"

Sid looked at McBride, and his eyes were troubled. "I was thinking that this was happening. When I get back to headquarters I have to give a full report to the station commander. He in turn has to report to the coroner. People will be called to give evidence. Me for one, and you too. Can you give me your address?"

"Of course." He pulled a business card from his pocket, turned it over took out a pencil and scribbled on the back. "This is the address I'm staying at in Sydney. I will be back later today. On the front is my mobile number, the printed address is my home in England."

"You can be certain the coroner will be in touch."

One of the fire crew came up to them. "Boss, there are graves over at the other side of the plot, in an orchard."

Sid, the crew captain said, "John, did you know that?"

"No. I think we ought to have a look." They both stood up from the grass near the fence and made the long detour round the end of the building and up the other side. Here the land was well cultivated. First they walked past rows of vegetables, peas, beans, potatoes until they arrived at the orchard. One or two trees close to the buildings had been fire-damaged, but the orchard in general had been untouched by the ravages of the night. The sun shone through the branches, casting dappled light on the grass beneath. In the center a row of mounds were lined up east to west. McBride could see that six bodies were buried. The last recently, the earth still a raw earthen mound unlike the other grassy knolls. At the head of each mound a wood lath stuck up vertically. On each peg a name was written in black felt tip. The earlier graves had words that were indecipherable. On the new grave, the name read: LUCY.

McBride stopped in front of it. Bowed his head and remembered the thin, bright girl. How hungry she had been. What a rotten life she must have had, only to die at such an early age. He prayed silently for a few moments.

Then he waved goodbye to the fire captain and slowly walked up the path to the road, and his parked car.

CHAPTER 7

The self-styled Reverend Pepper was sweating with fear. People killed last night that he had locked up in their bedrooms, unable to get out. He didn't know what would happen, but he did know that it wouldn't be pleasant, especially not for Christopher Pepper. Using his cell, he phoned the local taxi company in Dulong, booked a cab to collect him.

Still in the clothes he had on the previous evening, scorched and smelling of smoke, and unwashed, his face streaked with soot, he made his way along the track towards the road. He sat on the sign announcing the cult. And waited. Down by the ruin that had been the Children of Messiah church and home, a lone fire engine sat guarding the smoking ruin, two firemen looking on, ready to hose down any flames that might rise unbidden.

Pepper did not have long to wait. He saw the cab from more than a mile away making its way up the straight country road. He stood up, and walked forward to the edge of the road. The taxi slowed down, its winking indicator operating, and it turned into the track, and reversed out again, facing back to Dulong. The driver put his hand out of the window, opened the back door, which swung out to its full extent, due to the car's angle on the road camber. The sun gleamed on the wet tarmac, steam rose with the sun's heat.

Pepper climbed into the cab's rear compartment, pulling the door shut after himself. He settled into the seat, leaned forward to say to the driver: "Harold Fox's house. You know where it is?" The taxi driver nodded without speaking, looking into rearview mirror checking for traffic. He let the clutch in and moved off.

Pepper sat unmoving in the back of the cab, looking out of the window but seeing nothing. He was trying to think, but nothing came into his mind. He fell asleep, and then the taxi driver was shaking him, the cab door open, and the driver on the pavement perhaps afraid that he was dead. His eyes popped open, and awareness hit him suddenly. He was outside Harold's house. Groggily he emerged from the taxi, feeling in his pocket for money. He pulled a twenty out, and put it in the cabbie's hand. The driver shouted goodbye, but Pepper didn't answer. He was using all his attention and remaining energy climbing the grand flight of steps up to Harold's front door.

When at last he reached the porch, he leaned against the bell, and as the sound of it ringing inside reached him, he felt his eyes closing, and he was only pulled awake again when he stumbled and felt himself falling. At that moment the door suddenly opened. An old man looked at him. He was dressed in a dark suit, complete with white shirt and grey tie, shoes polished to a high shine.

Pepper said, "Is Mr. Fox in?"

"What name shall I say?" He was looking at Pepper with a grimace, obviously considering his appearance below contempt.

Ignoring the look, Pepper drew himself together and stepped over the threshold. "Tell him that the Reverend Christopher Pepper has called to give him important news." Then, uninvited, he collapsed into a side chair in the imposing hall.

The man turned, muttered something Pepper couldn't hear, and walked away across the hall and through one of many doors.

Pepper was asleep again when the man returned. His head was forward on his chest, and he was snoring softly. The man in the suit coughed loudly, and when that brought no results, shook Pepper vigorously. He woke with a start.

"I am sorry. I have been awake all night."

"Mr. Fox will see you now. Please follow me." They went through a door, and Harold Fox was sitting at a huge table eating breakfast, dressed in a tracksuit. Behind him were French windows leading to a large terrace, and below the terrace, extensive and well-tended gardens.

"Christopher," greeted Fox, not rising or stopping his breakfast, continuing to shovel bacon, eggs and sausages into his mouth. "Sit down at the table, and tell me what you are doing here so early, and so unkempt. Have you had an accident?"

Pepper pulled out a dining chair, and collapsed into it. "Last night, we had a lightning strike on the cult. The building has been totally destroyed. Thirteen people were killed, more may die. That is partly why I am distraught. Worse than that the fire brigade know that the girls were locked in their bedrooms. Can you imagine what this means not just for me, but for you too? We could well be charged with murder. A man called John McBride was at the scene as well."

Fox's mouth was open, astounded. All thoughts of his breakfast had vanished. "McBride? That artist guy that has been sniffing around last week? I don't believe it. Could he have set the place alight himself, to cause a scene?"

"No, it was a lightning strike. The roof went up like a roman candle. Those cheap linoleum tiles really burn. Didn't you know it was dangerous to use them?"

"It was a matter of using lightweight tiles. Slate or pan-tiles would have been too heavy. The contractor specified them. They weren't illegal forty years ago. And they've stood the test of time since."

"Until they killed a lot of people. We should start thinking of answers before people start asking the questions. The first thing the authorities will do is hold an inquest into the deaths. That is what they always do after a fire where there is loss of life. McBride was there as the fire started. He talked to the fire brigade chief. He will be called for a start."

"Where is he now?" Fox absently pushed the coffee pot in Pepper's direction across the table. Pepper got hold of it, and with some effort managed to lift it, and pour some coffee into the cup by his place setting. He drank greedily, black coffee, unsweetened. He could feel the energy being generated in him.

"I should think he has gone to the hotel here in Dulong. He, too, has been up all night. I don't think he would have the energy to drive back to Sydney."

Fox put down his knife and fork. They clattered on his plate. "Better get down to basics, young Pepper. Start with the urgent things that must be done."

Pepper interrupted him. "I am getting down to basics, thinking how to stop both of us being imprisoned for life."

Fox waved his arms about, shouted. "As we speak, the hospital may be discharging some of your girls, those that have not been injured in the fire. Where will they go? Where is their mentor when he is needed? You should be at the hospital waiting to gather in those that are being discharged, and visiting those that are bedridden. Get to it."

"Meanwhile, what will you be doing?"

"Speaking to the insurance company, arranging temporary accommodation. For starters. I think that we can hire caravans, pitch them down the track. Four residents to a caravan." He picked at his teeth with a pick removed from a small eggcup full of them, and thought for a moment. "You wouldn't need to pay any rent, because the insurance people would pay that for a while. Two years, I think. We'll have to look at the policy… think how many vans you would need, including one for yourself."

Fox stopped picking his teeth, absently picked up a slice of toast and took a bite out of it. "Have some toast, and then get down to the hospital. Get the doctors to hang on to the ones they are discharging until we can organize the caravans. Later today, say. I'll keep in touch on your cell phone. Off you go now."

Slice of toast in his hand, Pepper rose from his chair and still sleepy walked out of the door to do what Fox ordered.

Fox remained at the table and picked up a land line phone from the sideboard, where it sat in its charger, close enough for Fox to answer it. He knew the telephone number of his friend Charles who owned a caravan showroom and adjacent site.

When Charles answered Fox explained what had happened to the Children of Messiah building, and how he needed to rent a lot of caravans to house the homeless until the home could be rebuilt. "I think we would need about twelve delivered to site, probably on a six month term. Anyway, until we have the new building ready for occupation. I'm going to phone the insurance company now. You won't need to fret, they will pay." The deal was done, and Charles would get started right away, ferrying the vans to site. If he was short of numbers Charles would hire them elsewhere.

Then Harold Fox sat back in his dining chair, took a biscuit from the barrel on the table, nibbled at it while he thought about John McBride, and what would be sufficient punishment for his unwanted interference.

Chapter 8

McBride woke, lying in bed but not knowing for a few moments where he was. It was dark, but through the gaps in the curtain he could see light. Suddenly memory came flooding back. He was in Dulong and had arrived at the local hotel, indeed the only hotel in town that morning at seven. He got out of bed and drew the curtains back, looked at his watch on the bedside table. Twelve thirty. He had enjoyed five hours of unbroken sleep. He felt a lot better. He put on his clothes, the ones he had worn last night, smoke-stained, smelly clothes, but he had no others. When he came to Dulong he hadn't intended staying, so he had packed nothing. Before he left for Sydney, he had a couple of things to do. He went downstairs, rang the bell at the makeshift reception, and when a girl appeared, asked how much she wanted because he was leaving. She produced a bill, and he gave her some notes. Once outside he left the car on the road where he had parked it, and made for the police house up the street.

The clerk was behind the desk in the front room. "Sergeant Burrows, please," said McBride. The woman sniffed in disdain at the sight of his clothes, opened the door behind her, and shouted "Stan."

The sergeant came through the door from the inner office. "Oh, Mr. McBride, you look as though you've been in a fire."

"That's what I've come to talk to you about. The fire at the Children of Messiah."

"You don't want me. That is big time policing, they've sent a scene-of-crime bus from Sydney, fully staffed, parked up at the cult." McBride looked at the policeman, who seemed pleased that he wasn't able to help him. What a strange person. He turned and went out of the door without replying, walked back to the car, and climbed in.

Along at the cult site, it was all activity, Land Rovers pulling caravans on to the track by the burned out building. Parked on the verge in front of the sign was a large motor home. The signs on the side indicated that it had been converted: *Federal Police NSW*. The door in the body of the truck was open, swinging in the light breeze. McBride parked in front of the vehicle, walked back to the swinging door, knocked on it and climbed in.

A young policewoman's desk faced him. She was writing longhand in a ledger. At another desk, a man in shirtsleeves with his back to McBride and the door.

McBride spoke to the girl. "Good day, I was here last night, getting people out." At the sound of his voice, the man at the far desk swung round, and smiled.

"Well, well, hello Mr. McBride. Still investigating?" It was Sergeant Jack Hopkins from the police station in Sydney. He stood up and leaned across to shake his hand. "When I heard about this case, I thought, that name, the Children of Messiah, a guy only came in the other day talking about it. So I said to the boss could I go?"

"It wasn't me that started the fire," said McBride. "I saw the lightning strike, over this end gable. Then the tiles flared up and there was no way of stopping it, even if fire engines had been standing by. But you can give me some information. Presumably there will be an inquest on the people who died? Will I get called to give evidence? I hope I will. It was a terrible thing all those girls who couldn't get out."

"Have you given your name to anyone, if you were here?" Hopkins was already reaching across his desk for a pad.

"Yes, the Fire Brigade Crew Chief."

Hopkins turned to the girl at the desk. "Sally, you got the name John McBride on your list?" The girl turned the pages of her ledger.

"Yes, John McBride, and an address in Sydney. Note says he pulled out some people before the brigade got here."

Hopkins smiled. "There you are John, you are sure to be called. You anything else you want to tell us? You can sit over by my desk, if you want."

"I'll have a coffee if you're inviting, and I'll tell you a couple of things you might not know." McBride squeezed over to Hopkin's desk, and the policeman sat himself down with his pad laid on the desk in front of him. He picked up a pen, turned to Sally asked for two coffees, then turned back to McBride, pen poised and his eyebrows raised.

"Two things I wanted to tell you. First, all the bedroom doors were locked with the girls inside. We had to break the doors down, which delayed things, and certainly there would have been fewer deaths if the doors hadn't been locked. Secondly, I became aware, just before the fire started, that the building was being used as a brothel. There was a crowd of local fellows in the car park queuing for service. I would have thought it would have been well known in the area."

Hopkins sat back, sucking the end of his pen. "Your first statement, the locking of doors is very, very serious. As regards prostitution the law in New South Wales is very laid back. Brothels are legal under certain conditions, but not if the workers are coerced into the business. Might go either way, that. But I'll make a note. The women weren't under age?"

"I don't imagine so. As to coercion, as I understood from a telephone conversation with Lucy, who is dead I found out today, there was coercion. If they wouldn't take part in prostitution, then they didn't get fed. I think that was what she meant."

Hopkins looked grim, and made notes. Eventually he looked up. "I don't think anybody still alive will say they were coerced into prostitution. The girls will want to go back to live in the cult, they know no other life. If they complain about anything they stand a chance, they will think, of being abandoned." He stood up. "Did you see the graves down there?" he said, suddenly changing the subject.

McBride looked up at him. "Yes, Lucy's was one of them. The one without grass."

"I've had a quick word with the registrar for the area, and they haven't been notified of any deaths. You probably know that is an offense."

McBride said, "Well I've said what I came to say. I want to get back to Sydney before dark. You know where to get hold of me if you want."

When McBride had gone, Sergeant Hopkins looked up Harold Fox's telephone number in the local book. He dialed it himself, and Fox answered. He introduced himself and said that he wanted to interview him over the Children of Messiah fire. He could either come up to the scene-of-crime van on the site, or Hopkins could call at his house.

"Why, I want to come up there myself to see that all the temporary accommodation is satisfactory. I can be up there 'bout half an hour. Who do I ask for?"

"Sergeant Jack Hopkins."

When Harold Fox put the phone down, he said "*fuck it,*" to himself. He dialed Pepper on his cell phone. It was answered almost straight away. Fox could hear a vehicle revving its engine.

"Hey, Pepper, it's Fox here. Where are you?"

"At the Children's site. We're in the middle of locating the caravans. We will need some bedding, and all sorts of personal belongings, toothbrushes, soap, dresses, the list is endless. Who will be able to help on that?"

"I don't know. I'll have to think. I'm coming over to the site now, because the police want to question me. Have they questioned you?"

"No. They don't know who I am. You might recall I'm a bit of a mess since I was in the fire, I've lost my dog collar."

Or thrown it away thought Fox, but didn't say so. "Don't say anything, and I'll see you when I've finished talking to this Sergeant Hopkins. If you're asked plead smoke inhalation or something." *Like insanity*, thought Fox. He finished the call.

Harold Fox arrived at the Children of Messiah site, and parked his large Jaguar car in front of the police bus. He climbed out of the car's plush leather interior, the door closing with a satisfying *thunk* behind him. As he walked over to the bus, he cast an eye over the line of caravans down the track, and a sense of powerful satisfaction filled him. He climbed up into the police bus, his huge bulk blocking the daylight, which caused the police constable to look up from her ledger.

Fox said, "I'm here to see the sergeant, we spoke on the phone."

Hopkins swiveled his seat round. "Hello Mr. Fox, come over and take a seat."

Fox pushed his way with difficulty past the desks and took the proffered chair.

Hopkins took out his pen, and pulled a statement form in front of him. "We'll just jot down your particulars." He wrote down what Fox told him, name, address, date of birth. "So tell me Mr. Fox, how you became involved with the Children of Messiah." He sat back and waited.

"I decided to put something back. I earned quite a lot of money over the years. I built this building mostly by myself, after buying the land. 'course I had it designed by an architect. There were a lot of children who were in dreadful orphanages. I engaged a religious minister who taught the children free of charge. When the kids grew up, they stayed on, growing food, tending animals. In that way it became almost self-supporting, together with some charitable donations. I had a few people looking after the kids, and they stayed on after the kids grew up." He smiled, "The kids called them their guarding angels."

"Then I got the cancer, and left to live in Dulong, where I could get treatment. A reverend gentleman, used to be a Mormon, he lived here, ran the cult, paid me a bit of rent for me to live on. I don't often come here, but I advise Mr. Pepper when he requires it. Today, I organized these caravans for the members to live in while we rebuild."

Hopkins looked at him thoughtfully. "You grew up in this area?"

"Yes, that's right. You must know that I got a three-year jail term for rape. Lots of people know that, not just the police. I didn't come back to this area for years, until I'd made some money."

"You set up the cult, populated it with young girls. Are you a pedophile, Mr. Fox?"

"I object to that. I have no sexual feelings at all. The cancer ended all thoughts of sex, I had radiotherapy for a tumor of the prostate. The hospital also accidently treated my testicles. I don't tell many people that, so I'd be obliged if you keep it confidential."

"I'll rephrase the question," Hopkins said, "before you had prostate cancer, were you a pedophile?"

"The answer is no." He had his fingers crossed beneath the desk.

"How much are you paid by the cult? The rent, how much?"

Fox looked at him for a time, the said, "I won't answer that, you've overstepped the line, young man." John Hopkins didn't look embarrassed. He merely inverted the form he had filled in so that Fox could read it.

"When you've read that, please could you sign where indicated?" He held out his pen. Fox took it, scanned the document, and then signed it. "You are free to go,"

said the policeman. "Oh, just a moment, something else I want to ask you. When you ran the cult, did you lock the orphans in their rooms at night?"

Fox stood up. "We locked the outside doors is all, so the kids didn't get outside. I think people living at home with kids do that as well." He turned and made his way out of the motor bus. He left his car where it was, and walked down the track to find Pepper. As he made his way down the track, the sergeant stood at the window and watched him. The scene out of the window was dominated by the blackened skeleton of the burned out building.

"Pepper!" shouted Fox, spotting him talking to one of the van drivers. Pepper

turned round and waved.

CHAPTER 9

Harold Fox waved Pepper into one of the caravans and said, "We shouldn't be seen talking together. The copper is looking out of his bus window. We'll be okay in here for a moment. I would like you to come up to my house later on. First go into town and get the supplies you need. If you plead poverty with one of the stores you should get a good discount. Get them to ship it down straight away, and then come to my house. Look at the first floor, if the lights are on, come and knock on my door. If you don't see them on go away back to the cult site. What I'm trying to do is stop you being interviewed until I've talked to you. Okay, you got that?"

Pepper looked all in, almost in a state of collapse. He nodded, and sat down at the table in the caravan to make out a list of supplies needed for the Children of the Messiah. Fox came out of the caravan and trudged back up the track to his car.

***

Pepper never arrived at Fox's house that night, and Fox couldn't raise him on the phone. He thought maybe that the police had taken him in, maybe he was in the cells. He was minded to phone Stan Burrows to check, but quickly put the thought out of his head. He would only stir things up if he wasn't in custody. He would phone him again tomorrow morning. He had been tired when he saw him last, then he had to go for supplies, and the girls would be leaving the hospital and occupying the caravans. Even Fox realized that a tired man might just fall into his bed and go out like a light.

Fox was up early the next morning, and the first thing he did, even before breakfast, was dial Pepper's number. This time he got a reply, Pepper sounding brisk and business-like.

"Good morning to you," said Fox. "You got time to come up to my house? I'm assuming you haven't been interviewed yet?"

"No. And yes, I'll be at your house in half an hour."

"Look to see the lights on upstairs, but I don't expect any problems." *Time for breakfast before he's here*, thought Fox.

Breakfast over, Fox was busy reading the morning newspaper when he heard the doorbell. He waited until his man brought Pepper through. Pepper looked a changed person, colour in his cheeks, new suit complete with dog collar, ever the God-fearing man. Outwardly, at least.

Fox folded his paper, laid it on the side table. "Right, Pepper, let's get down to business. It's urgent. We've got to agree the story." Pepper sat down unbidden on the comfy chair opposite, folded his arms expectantly.

"When the police interviewed me, it was obvious what they wanted: who locked the girls in their bedrooms, were the girls forced to carry out prostitution against their will, and what about the bodies of girls buried in the grounds? Well, give me honest answers first. Then we'll decide what we say."

"I think girls were being locked up before I took over. Also, the system was that the girls didn't get fed if they wouldn't have sex. As for the bodies, the only one we buried on my watch was Lucy, who died about a week ago."

Fox said, "This guy McBride, who I've heard all about was involved in dragging people from the fire. I heard he found the bedroom keys in your pocket, Pepper. As to the bodies, they will dig them up, do autopsies and discover the truth. Let that be your truth too, Pepper."

"She didn't want to eat and she got ill. We prayed for her every day, but the good Lord decided to take her."

Fox grimaced. "You should have sent her to the hospital, they will say."

"There seemed nothing wrong with her except she didn't want to eat."

Fox was silent for a while, running scenarios through his mind. "You might get away with it, on the grounds that you are a religious nut," he conceded. "But you stand the risk of concealing a death."

"There were other people buried on the site. I will say I thought it was a legal burial ground."

"Not a good excuse. What about locking the girls in their rooms?"

"I'll say I didn't lock anyone in their rooms. It must have been someone else. One of the staff."

"As I said, Pepper, I heard that McBride got the keys from your pocket."

"All the keys were on a ring in my pocket. Keys to fit every damn lock in the building. Lots of people would have duplicates."

"Yes, that's a good answer, might get you off the hook. But don't swear like you just did. People might doubt you're a reverend in reality."

Fox yawned, even though it wasn't even late morning. He thought the guy in front of him was a big bore, enough to make anyone yawn. He said, "What we gotta do is get rid of McBride. We don't want him spouting off to the coroner, and that's what he's intent on. Don't forget he was on the scene. And he'd been doing some detective work beforehand, too."

Pepper looked startled. "Surely we're not going to kill him? What would we do with the body, bury it?"

"No, no. That would be stupid, and dangerous. Murderers get put away for life. We just have to get him out of the way. I have an idea, it came to me yesterday. You know there's a lot of offshore islands, uninhabitable ones? We could stick him on one of those. Might never get found, ever.

"You won't know, but I have a boat. Small yacht, really. We might invite him over to it, under some assumed name. Once we've got him aboard, wouldn't be hard to slip him a drugged drink, motor out to one of these islands off Melbourne, drop him off. Wouldn't be found for years – if ever. If he isn't around, they can't call him as a witness. He doesn't know me personally, hasn't met me."

"Sounds okay," said Pepper, sounding dubious.

"Even better, McBride is due to give his next exhibition in Melbourne. He'll be waiting for a call. His agent has gone back to England, will come back for the Perth show. I'll phone him pretend to be the agent from Melbourne, get him to visit my boat."

"How do you get to know all these things?"

"I don't just sit on my ass. I do research, talk to people. You don't know the half of it."

Harold Fox quickly got rid of Reverend Pepper, and settled down in his study to do some research. First he searched the internet for commercial art galleries in Melbourne, and made a list complete with telephone numbers. He spent half an hour phoning, and found out that John McBride would be having an exhibition of his water colours starting in a couple of months at the Laurel Gallery in the city.

Next he phoned the gallery in Sydney that he knew had the McBride art show currently running. He asked if he might speak to Mr. McBride. The lady on the phone said she was sorry, but he wasn't in the gallery today. However, she had a cell phone number for him that she could let him have. Fox thanked her profusely.

Now Fox was going to take a chance, but thought it was well worth it. He would impersonate a Mr. Peterson who he had spoken to at the Laurel Gallery.

He made the call, and McBride picked his cell phone. Harold Fox impersonated Peterson quite well. It may not have been necessary, maybe McBride had never spoken to him before.

"Hello Mr. McBride. It's the Laurel Gallery in Melbourne here, Petersen speaking. I just thought I should make contact with you, I know your agent is back in England for a few weeks. How did your exhibition go in Sydney?"

"Quite well. I'm looking forward to painting in Melbourne shortly, and meeting you."

"Actually that's why I phoned. I would like it if you can come over this weekend. Either by rail or by air, and I can meet you, and take you down to the harbour where I have a boat. We can have a few drinks and eats, talk about our upcoming exhibition. How about it?"

"That's very kind of you, Mr. Petersen. I think I'd rather fly out. I looked at train travel, and it's kind of slow."

"Quite so, I always fly myself."

"I'll come over, maybe spend a week or two, get some painting done of the Melbourne area. Can you fix me up with an apartment or otherwise book me into a four star hotel. I'll come out tomorrow, Saturday. Will that be okay for you?"

"It certainly will be, I'll make the arrangements, email you with the flight details, too. I think I've got your email details somewhere."

"Well, thank you so much I look forward to seeing you tomorrow."

Fox wiped the sweat off his brow. The email business was a no-no. It would lead directly to him when McBride disappeared. He would fix the details then phone him back, saying he had mislaid his email. He didn't want that raising again it had been careless of him, and had nearly blown it at the first hurdle. It could still go wrong. If, for example, McBride were to phone the real Mr. Petersen. God almighty.

Fox phoned Pepper, told him what was planned, that he would want his help all the following day. Best that he came down say eight in the morning to Fox's own house, but not wearing a dog collar under any circumstances. Best to wear casual clothes and sand shoes or trainers, because they would be going on a cruise.

Next Fox sat down at his desk to plan out the following day. He could manage to sail his cruiser single handed to the island he planned to drop McBride off at. He would spike McBride's drink. With Pepper's assistance they would land McBride.

It was a pity that there would be a trail leading to Melbourne, and an unoccupied hotel room. Things could go wrong, but he would have to take the chance.

CHAPTER 10

Fox was up bright and early the following day. As soon as Pepper arrived at his house, true to instructions in a pair of blue denims, sports shirt, open necked, and a pair of sand shoes, Fox shoveled him into his car, and made the trip down to the marina, and introduced him to his boat, a fifty foot motor cruiser, sea-going fiberglass hull and wood superstructure. He took Pepper aboard, showed him the layout, and where Pepper was going to hide and get the drinks ready for when Fox returned to the boat with McBride together with the preparation of some nibbles to accompany the drinks. Fox kept the spike pills for the drink in his pocket. He didn't trust Pepper to identify the right drink for McBride. If left to Pepper, it might be Fox himself lying unconscious on deck. Under no circumstances was Pepper to show his face in McBride's company, because of course McBride would recognize him from the occasion of the fire at the Children of Messiah site.

Next Fox drove his Jaguar saloon up to the airport to meet McBride. He carried with him a cardboard placard with McBride's name on it, but thought that in, any case he would recognize McBride from photos he had seen. Fox was just in time, because as he entered the airport, McBride's plane was on its final approach. He left his car in the short term car park, and was at the gate several minutes before the passengers turned up. McBride was last out, pulling a trolley piled with cases and painting gear, and smiling at Fox, who was holding the placard up.

"Sorry I was late. The bloody carousels always get stuck when I'm around. Still, I've got everything."

Fox smiled. "Welcome to Melbourne, we're having a good spell of weather."

He turned and led McBride down to the car, and filled the boot with his luggage. He opened the front passenger door and McBride climbed in. Fox got into the driving seat and started off for the downtown Marriott. He got McBride checked in and his luggage unloaded. Then they were off again heading for the marina.

"Do you like living in Melbourne?" said McBride, probably just to make conversation.

"Sure," said Fox, "It's a vibrant community, have you noticed that all Australian cities are on the coast? Except for Canberra of course. I'd hate to live there. When we needed a capital city here, and no-one could agree to allow one of the existing cities to have the honour, it was decided to build the city of Canberra. They made a real pig's ear of it. For a long time, there was a huge lake in the middle of it, but they didn't get around to filling it."

"All fairly modern there, isn't it?" said McBride. "I haven't been, but I read the book by Bill Bryson, you know, the American author."

"Yes, I know," said Fox, getting bored by the polite conversation. Fortunately the marina came into view ahead, with something else to talk about.

"My word," said McBride when he saw the marina for the first time, the lines of boats stretching out it seemed, into the horizon. "There's a few million dollars in the water there."

"Yes, it's not a cheap hobby."

They drew up opposite Fox's boat, and got out. McBride spotted the name but said nothing, just tucked the information away in his mind. *Speedy Fox* was the name on the transom. The name Fox, and the connection with Dulong. Yes, he had it. The owner of the cult building. The garage owner came into his mind, laughing as he told McBride the story of Harold Fox.

Fox, despite his ungainly bulk stepped aboard the boat with agility, turned to McBride who was just stepping aboard, and said, "I've got my man aboard, getting some nibbles ready, and some drinks. Sit down there," pointed to a table and chairs under the aft awning, "and I'll be right back." He disappeared down the companionway, shutting the door behind him. *Funny, why is he shutting me out?* thought McBride. But he did as told, and sat himself down, looking out at the marina, comparing boats. At this side, were medium sized boats, fifty footers most of them. Across the other side, he could see the opulent yachts, hundred foot and bigger. He looked down over the gunwale, and in the clear water, saw masses of fish swimming, some of them a couple of feet long.

He heard the door latch click, and Fox emerged carrying a tray, which he put down on the table. On the tray, were bowls of finger snacks, nuts, biscuits, and olives.

"Back again in a minute," said Fox and disappeared below. When he returned, it was with glasses, a bottle of gin, and one of whisky. He also had a bowl of ice cubes.

He stood in front of the table. "What's your tipple, Mr. McBride?"

"Whisky on the rocks will be fine."

Fox turned his back to McBride, who heard the glugging of the whisky bottle, and the clunk of ice cubes against the glass.

Fox already had the pill in his hand, and he had put it in the glass, before pouring the whisky. By the time he added the ice, and stirred the concoction, the pill had dissolved. Fox poured himself a gin, without a tablet, and put both glasses on the table, one in front of McBride, one in front of himself.

He sat down and said, "Bottoms up!" taking a huge drink from his glass. McBride, he was pleased to see, drank hugely, too. In a few minutes, Fox was replenishing both glasses. Two minutes later, he saw McBride trying to speak and failing. Another two minutes and McBride was asleep in his chair, snoring.

Fox lost no time in opening the companionway door and shouting for Pepper. When his head popped through the opening Fox said, "Up forward and cast off." Fox himself cast off aft, and started the engines. Within a minute they were leaving the marina.

The island where they were going to abandon McBride was twelve miles offshore and several miles up-coast from the marina. The motor yacht had a fair turn of speed and was soon doing thirty knots through a choppy sea, battling against the trade wind.

The uninhabited island came up on the horizon, one of a chain stretching along the coast. It had been a prison island in the eighteenth century, long since disbanded as being too expensive to run, and after nearly a century of disuse all that was visible of past habitation was a stubby pier on the lee side, and the remains of a brick building, gaunt against the sky.

Fox eased back on the throttle once he was in the lee of the island. The sea was smooth here, and on engine tick-over, the boat slid over the clear water, heading for the remainder of the pier which had long since lost its wooden extension and was now just a stone rectangle barely reaching the sea at low tide. Now the tide was nearly full and Fox was able to edge the boat and come about parallel with the shoreline, a fender chafing the stone wall. Fox dropped anchor, and Pepper and he picked up McBride, Fox taking his shoulders, Pepper his legs. They manhandled him down the short pier, and laid him on the shingle. His eyes were open by this time, but he just laid there, seemingly paralyzed.

As the *Speedy Fox* upped anchor and moved away from the island, Pepper said, "He will be all right, won't he?" Fox looked backwards.

"Why do you care?"

"I'm a Minister of God." Pepper looked as though he were seeing the real Harold Fox for the first time, and not liking what he saw.

Chapter 11

McBride stared up at the cloudless blue sky wondering where he was. He couldn't move even though he tried. He was paralyzed, although it didn't alarm him. His brain still worked, and had been working since he had regained consciousness. He remembered being laid down in the open air. He smelled the sea on the breeze that swept over him. Presumably he was lying on the beach. He knew that he had been given a spiked drink. As the men laid him down, he recognized the face of the man Pepper, the reverend of the Children of Messiah, although he was not wearing his dog collar. He knew if he was patient he would recover. He closed his eyes.

He woke slowly, and judging by the sun's position he had slept for maybe three hours. The feeling of nausea had gone. He stretched out an arm, felt sand and pebbles. He sat up carefully. His head was clear, no dizziness. He put both hands on the beach and levered himself up. He stood upright, cured as far as he could tell. He was hungry, so maybe he had slept longer than he thought.

This was like being back in the SAS, the crack British army regiment that even preceded the front line. The first thing they used to do was a recce to find out whether they could live off the land. This was an island. It had to be. What was the use of dropping him off on the coast where he could find civilization. A desert island presumably, but not one which had always been uninhabited. The ruined building nearby, and the pier he had been carried off the boat on told otherwise.

He would start his exploration by circumnavigating the coastline. When he arrived back here, he would explore the brick ruin, and strike away from the coast. He smiled to himself. Army teaching, once learned, always practiced.

He set off aiming to walk at a steady three miles an hour; that would give him some idea as to the size of his territory. The beach he was left on ran north to south. He could see to one side, in the distance what looked like a great mass of land. Australia itself, it seemed. So that would be north. He started out in a westerly direction, thereby going clockwise. This was for no rational reason, just the way his brain worked.

After a mile, the coastline was veering west, and he was facing into a stiff wind, undoubtedly the roaring forties, as the trade wind had long ago been named by transcontinental sailors. Almost immediately he was climbing what turned out to be a cliff. Underfoot was closely cropped grass. The most likely animal to be eating the grass short would be rabbits. Very edible if not too easy to catch without traps of some sort. By now he had climbed about forty or fifty feet, and he stopped to look down the cliff. He was on a rocky outcrop, but the cliff hadn't risen sheer from the sea, but in haphazard steps of a sedimentary rock, weathered into slabs that broke off with the pounding of the waves. Out to sea, rocks were jutting out of the sea. McBride, thinking food, knew that an excursion at low tide would probably reveal spider crabs, and shellfish such as mussels, and if he was lucky, oysters. So far the food stocks seemed assured. As he walked there were lots of seabirds, both on the steps of the cliff, where they had built nests. The birds landed and took off from the top of the low cliff totally ignoring McBride. They had no fear, and as a result McBride considered them as another food source. The eggs would be very tasty he knew. The birds themselves he had to be careful of, most gulls were scavengers. Depending how far he was from civilization, the gulls might be feeding from land fill sites, and that could be bad. In any case, adult birds could taste very fishy due to their diets. Young birds were best, and especially if only the breasts were eaten. The worry was fresh water. He recalled that the climate around Melbourne was a fairly high rainfall area, so maybe he would be okay.

He was descending now to sea level. He looked over to the center of the island, and thought it wasn't much higher than the cliff he had climbed. Ahead of him there was some bush and small trees. As he got nearer he saw to his amazement that the wood comprised mainly apple trees, and most of the trees had hanging fruit. He went over to one of the trees to examine the fruit. He picked one of the apples, the ripest one within reach. It looked quite attractive and he took a small bite. The flesh was white against the green skin, and not too sour. He munched on it, sitting at the base of the tree and looking out to sea. That was when he saw the boat. It was a thirty footer motor launch with two people in it, a man and a girl. They were heading in what McBride thought was the direction of Melbourne. McBride quickly took off his shirt, stood up and waved his shirt in the air, jumping up and down. After a moment the people in the boat looked over to the island and saw him. He saw the man pointing him out to the girl. They waved back, but didn't slacken speed. He stood and watched them until they were a tiny blot on the horizon.

Disappointed, he went and picked a dozen more apples and stuffed them in his pockets. He pulled his shirt on again to avoid sunburn.

Before long he had reached a long shallow beach, with mighty rollers breaking on the sand, and spume whipped by the wind. It was the furthest extremity of the island to the west. He cut across to the north, and once across the expanse of the sands, he could see the Australian mainland in the distance. He still he made it twelve miles. Facing east again, with the wind on his back, low hills appeared in front of him, this time there were tiny V-shape valleys, which McBride studied. He concluded that they were caused by water run-off from the hill top. The rainfall must be higher than he at first imagined. Again there were rocky cliffs. Or maybe they were too small to be termed cliffs. Eventually, McBride could see the derelict building in the distance. He began looking at his watch from time to time, and he was coming up with the figure of three hours or nine miles circumference, and it was nearly circular. About six and one half square miles. He should be able to live self-sufficiently here all his life. How boring that would be. This was day one. He reckoned he would be back on the mainland in seven days, tops. Already he was thinking about building a raft. To swim twelve miles in a rough shark-infested sea did not appeal. He had read about the sharks in the oceans here.

He reached the old broken down building and there on the side he approached a pool about twenty feet diameter, and inland from it a short stream with water bubbling up from underground. Wow, an underground spring! Whether it was fed only by the water collected on the hill top, or from a deeper aqueduct maybe emanating from the mou788ntains on the mainland he did not know or care. He went down on his knees, and put his hand in the water, scooping enough to taste. It was as fresh as could be.

Over in the broken down building was a jumble of debris. He looked up before entering, frightened that the structure may be on the point of collapse. But as he looked up he saw that the front of the building had been removed at some time, maybe in an attempt at reconstruction. What remained seemed to be in no immediate danger of collapsing any further. The floor on the first level had dropped to the ground at the front, but was still in its original place at the back. It rested at forty-five or fifty degrees. It was only part of the first floor, maybe a third of the width. If he could get it out of the building, McBride reasoned that it might be the framework of a largish raft. But he wasn't going to start today. He needed a meal, and a fire to cook it on. He looked up at the sun, still well above the horizon. In his pocket he had a penknife, the sort that some people would label a scout knife. It was very useful for his painting work.

He pulled it out of his pocket now, and pried from one side a small magnifying glass. The high tide mark was a jumble of seaweed. He knew it was dry.

It crunched under his shoes. He knelt and selected pieces of weed, built it into a loose pile focused the glass. And waited. Within seconds a white column of smoke rose from the seaweed. A couple of minutes later, and flames crackled and leaped. McBride piled on more seaweed, searched around for twigs and small dead branches. Soon he had a bonfire going.

He went back into the derelict building, searching for pieces of wood, and found broken pieces of furniture. Whilst he was doing this he came across a metal bowl, black with age, a bit like a dog bowl. He hoped it hadn't been, took it round to the fresh water pool, washed it as best he could.

The fire burned robustly, and he thought he had time to collect some sea bird eggs from the cliff just around the shore. He was careful not to take all the eggs from any one nest. The birds were agitated, and flew about flapping their wings in his face. He had the metal bowl with him, and placed the eggs in that.

He carried the bowl back to the freshwater pond, filled the bowl by submerging it. Reaching in to the bowl, he placed the eggs on the side of the pond. He left them there and took the bowl back, placed it on the fire with water still in it. He went back for the eggs, put them in his pockets to carry them back to the fire. When he got back, the water was bubbling, and he gently broke eggs on the bowl side, and dropped the contents into the water. Poached eggs for tea, and an apple for dessert. McBride was lucky that most of the eggs were newly laid, only one had a fetus, which he discarded.

When he had eaten, he laid down on the sand by the fire, using his folded jacket as a pillow. The sun was setting, and McBride was weary and soon asleep.

CHAPTER 12

Sergeant John Hopkins was in his office at the Federal Police Station in Sydney. He had returned from Dulong the previous evening. Hopkins' site work was completed, but the forensics were digging up the bodies in the orchard graveyard, shielded by large tents.

The superintendent bustled into Hopkins' office.

"Give me a rundown on how the Children of Messiah case is going."

"Well, I've finished my bit, got statements from the people who were on site during the fire, and also the owner of the building, Harold Fox. It's really waiting for the forensics, and then we can give all the lot over to the coroner. I've got an appointment with him later today."

"I think you ought to have Fox and Pepper in and put them on twenty-eight day bail. That will allow their passports to be taken away. You could also ask for daily reporting to a police station. If you don't do that, I think Fox will go abroad."

"Come on Sir, let me in on the secret. I can't do my job without all the info, even if it's hearsay."

"You're right," said the super, "one of my grasses has been contacted by Fox, who apparently is trying to realize his assets, right down to his house. My contact thinks he's ready to do a runner. Also, he's not asking for cash but gold, silver or gems. Apparently only at a push will he take US dollars."

"Right, Sir, we'll have them pulled in today. I'll take an officer with me, and we'll include the local man in Dulong. After all, Fox and Pepper will have to report to him."

Before going to Dulong, Hopkins made an appointment with the coroner, a man called Don Smith, an amiable fifty-year-old. He had met him in the past on a few cases. They sat at his desk, and Hopkins took out a cardboard-covered file with NSW Federal Police printed across the cover. In the space for the title it said: Case Number 534-17 Fire at Children of Messiah building. Smith took the file, put it on the desk in front of him, and looked up at Hopkins.

"I read about this case in the newspapers. A lot of people killed."

"We want the coroner's review opened fairly quickly, but it might have to be adjourned if a couple of people don't turn up. However, we are going to remand them. We will have to bail them, although we will keep their passports, and they will have to report daily."

"Off the record you know the suspects, but think they'll scarper."

Hopkins grimaced. "You've got the drift. Will you be able to open the proceedings beginning of next week? They're still digging up bodies on the site. The autopsy reports will be in a separate report later."

Smith made a notation on the file cover, put it into his in-tray. "I'll start reading it today." He stood up and Hopkins got the message. He stood up too and shook hands.

Back at the station, he collected a police constable, and together they made their way to the car-pen and booked out a car. They were in Dulong before lunch.

They parked outside Dulong police station, went in and asked to speak to Stan Burrows. The police constable popped his head round the door to his office.

"Come in. You're earlier than you said you would be."

"Yeah, we had a good run through," said Jack Hopkins. "This is Constable Rex Brown. Rex this is Stan Burrows."

The introductions over, they all sat round Stan's desk while Jack Hopkins told the other two the story.

Stan said, "We're going to pull them in today?"

"That's the idea. No time to waste. We'll start with Harold Fox. Will he be at home?"

"Should be, he doesn't go far these days."

Hopkins stood up, pushed the chair back, "Then let's go."

As they trouped out through the front office, Burrows said to the girl, "We'll be back shortly."

Burrows got into the front passenger seat so that he could show Hopkins the way to Fox's house. "Got your cuffs?" Hopkins asked.

"You're joking, yes?"

Hopkins shook his head, "No. He might be reluctant to come back to the station."

Burrows didn't reply, his lips a tight narrow line.

They pulled the police car in front of the steps, and walked up three abreast. Hopkins rang the bell. A mature man in a dark suit answered the door. "Police. We're here to see Harold Fox." He flipped his badge as he spoke. The man looked down at it.

"I'll ask if Mr. Fox will see you. If you will just wait in the hall." He closed the door when they were inside. Hopkins caught Rex Brown's eye, and smiled.

The man was gone for close on five minutes, and Hopkins was feeling that maybe Fox had already left, maybe in a car. Christ, he didn't need a car chase. Then a door opened and the man was back.

"If you will step this way, gentlemen." He led them into a large living room, French windows across the room looking down on to mature gardens, more like those laid out by Capability Brown, though Hopkins was sure he had never been to Australia in his life. An oldish man eased himself out of a chair as a mark of respect, though it didn't show in his face.

He saw Burrows, and said: "What's all this about, Stan?"

"The sergeant will tell you."

Hopkins knew then whose side Stan was on. He would need watching. Though surely he couldn't risk his job. He would need his pension in not many years now.

"We're going to charge you in connection with the fire and deaths at the cult. We will need your passport. We will bail you when you have had the charges officially made, but you will have to give us your passport and report once a day to the local station." He saw the shock it was causing Fox. That had caught him off guard. "So, Mr. Fox, if you will just fetch your passport, and a coat if you think you'll need one. We shan't keep you more than an hour, I wouldn't think. Just a few forms to fill in."

On the way out, the servant was standing in the hall as they filed past.

Fox said to him, "I'm just going out with these gentlemen, I will be home for dinner."

"Very good, Sir." The servant opened the outside door for them.

At the police station it was a tight fit to get everybody into Stan's office, and Stan and Rex stood against the wall. Fox sat opposite Hopkins at the desk. Hopkins had brought all the forms with him, and he quickly completed them as Fox gave the required information. Then Fox put his signature to the document, and was given the copy form. Fox handed over his passport, and stood up.

"Am I free to go now?"

"Yes, but don't forget to report in every evening at six. If you don't Stan will collect you, bring you in and bang you up."

Stan got the girl to drive Fox back in Stan's police car. Hopkins said, "Now we've got to go and pick up Pepper. Or maybe we could phone him and ask him to get his ass down here, what do you think?" He looked up at Stan who was still leaning against the wall.

Stan looked down at his watch, four o'clock. "Could try, if we knew his cell number, and if he isn't screwing one of his girls."

"You don't know his number?"

"Before the fire I didn't need to know. I had his landline number, but it's out of action, cos of the fire."

Hopkins said nothing, began to search his brie case, pulled out the statement by Pepper he'd taken yesterday. *Shit, the number he'd put down was a landline.*

"Okay, we'll go pick him up." And Hopkins led the way out.

On the way out Stan said, "We'll have to lock up the shop."

"Yeah, can't be helped. You could transfer calls to your cell. Couldn't you?" Hopkins looked at Stan and saw in his expression that he didn't know how to do that. "Well, doesn't matter. Come on."

The car drew up on the grass verge of the road just past the track. Big yellow construction machines and trucks were busy demolishing and hauling away the charred remains of the Children building. The tents were still erected over the graves. The caravans had been tidied up, positioned now in a long rank. Twelve caravans, Hopkins counted. Outside a lot of them, girls, or rather young ladies were sitting on the ground in groups talking. You could hear the sound of high voices even up here on the road. They saw some girls in the vegetable garden working, but it had taken a bit of a bettering during the fire, with firemen's boots doing most of the damage.

"Pepper's van is the first one," said Stan. And that was the one they knocked on. The women sitting around turned to look. Then the door opened and Pepper peered out. He had his shirt and trousers on, complete with dog collar. When they got inside the van they could see that he was alone. Stan was wrong about one thing.

Hopkins spoke, while he fiddled with his case, opening it on the table.

"You're probably wondering why we've come. We've already seen Fox, and charged him. Now we are charging you similarly." They went through the same rigmarole pointing out that he had to report every evening to the local police, and that he must give his passport to the police now.

"I haven't got a passport. It expired, and I never go abroad now." Hopkins arched his eyebrows and looked at Stan." He said, "Don't look at me. I've no idea."

Hopkins pulled out his cell phone, dialed. He asked to be put through to records, and when they answered said, "Sergeant Hopkins here. I want you to check on a man called Pepper, Christopher. He says he has no passport. Is he telling the truth? Address? Yeah, Children of Messiah near Dulong." He stood there with phone still to his ear, waiting. After five minutes, he said, "That's fine, it agrees with his reply."

Pepper looked at him. "See, I said I didn't have a passport."

"We had to check."

CHAPTER 13

McBride opened his eyes and immediately knew where he was. On the island on day two. Only five days left to build a raft and get back to Sydney.

The fire was out, but he could get it going again because the sun was shining. He stood up and stretched. He took off all his clothes, folded them and placed a rock on top. Then he ran down the beach and into the water. When the water was deep enough he started to swim, not out to sea, but along the beach. This was not exploration but exercise. Eventually he turned and swam back to his clothes feeling ready to face the day. He dried himself off by jogging over to the freshwater pool, taking his cooking pot with him. He filled the pot, had a long drink, and whilst he crouched there he saw something that grew along the opposite bank. Not lush growth but patchy scrubby plants. He recognized them as potato. But he couldn't dig them up with his bare hands. He needed an implement. He decided to look in the ruined building.

It was bright sunlight outside, but once he got inside the gloom enveloped him, and he scrabbled around by feel, forcing himself between the ground and the first floor which had fallen and was resting on the ground floor at the front, and still apparently attached to the back wall at first floor level. He edged towards the back wall, and could vaguely see a lot of interesting debris very vaguely. He crawled further under the forty degree floor. He heard a rumbling sound above him. He crouched lower and held his breath. He stayed motionless for five minutes, though breathing again. No further sound came. He looked upwards, carefully moving his body to do so. Something had moved and now was within hand's reach, and towards the daylight. As he strained his eyes, what he had first feared was a human body, turned out to be a large barrel. It had obviously been dislodged when the floor slipped, and had rolled down to the floor where McBride lay.

A barrel! Suddenly McBride was crawling out, looking to see if he could see other barrels in there. Barrels gave a raft buoyancy. The upper floor, if it could be detached and dragged out of the building, would work fine as the base of a raft. Four, or even six barrels would give it buoyancy. Add a mast and a rudimentary lee board and it would sail in the trade wind to the mainland. If he could find a sail.

What he did find was a spade. He was rummaging for rope at the time, and feeling hunger growing inside him. So the discovery was a big happy event. He went outside, waving the spade above his head. He collected the cooking bowl and ran round to the end of the drinking pond. He plunged the spade into the ground, and gently levered it out. The soil wasn't as compacted as had imagined. Once the spade was removed, he saw that it was sandy soil, and lying in the hollow left by the spade were two delicious looking potatoes. He dropped them into the cooking pot, and dug some more until he had a full bowl. He washed them in the pool, took them back to the beach in the bowl. He had an idea, and took the bowl down to the sea, and filled it with seawater. Add a bit of salt to the meal. He lit the fire with the magnifying glass, sat down and waited until the potatoes were done, added three eggs. He ate with his hands, and afterwards ate an apple. A perfect brunch, and he was ready for work.

Using the spade as a crowbar, he attacked the floor and managed to get it loose from the back wall. It came down suddenly and with a fair bit of noise. McBride jumped backwards quickly and avoided a painful death. When the dust had settled, and some small debris he could see that the floor planks had settled suspended, fairly level about two to three feet above the sand.

McBride got hold of the forward edge, and pulled with all his weight. He expected it not to move. So he was very surprised to find it rolling, yes, rolling out. He let go and the floor stopped rolling. He knelt down on the sand and looked underneath. The floor was resting on several more barrels, all the same size. He sat down and thought. Should he start the raft building above the high water line, or below? He favored just above, and saving some barrels to be able to roll the completed vessel afloat. He decided to check how many barrels there were in total. That would be the decider. He hunkered down on the sand, started counting the barrels under the floorboards. An amazing five. Then he went back to the building. Light flooded in, now that the collapsed floor was removed. A lot of brick debris. He really should clear that first, and then search. He started on the bricks, throwing them clear so that they piled up on either side of the building. He made no attempt to stack them neatly. Working from front to back was revealing useful objects. Wood working tools, including saws hung on the nearside wall. More shovels and gardening tools were leaning against the walls. A cupboard gradually unearthed from the bricks, turned out to contain boxes of nails and screws, drill bits. Somewhere there must be a hand drill, but certainly no electric tools. This dated before the twentieth century. There were also four more barrels. That settled the matter; he would build just above the high water line.

All this clearing of what was a large space left him weary by the middle of the afternoon, as he estimated it. His watch had become detached from his wrist at some time over the last two days.

He felt hungry enough to eat a couple of gulls, so he walked up the south side of the island to the cliffs.

He saw that the tide was at probably the lowest point. The rocks at the foot of the cliffs were exposed, and surrounded by shingle with enticing rock pools. He scrambled down the cliffs, and over to the nearest rock pool. He knelt down and pulled at seaweed to see if he could disturb any sea creatures. Crabs scurried away from him. He plunged his hands in the pools and managed to pull a couple out, with only one nasty nip to show for it. He took a large stone and killed each of them by striking the front of the shell. He left them on top of a prominent rock, and scrambled further to more interesting features. There was the skeleton of an old shipwreck, and clinging to the timbers: mussels. He wrenched a handful of shells, pushing them into his jacket pockets. His clothing was a mess by now, after his clearance of the old building. Sleeping on the beach hadn't helped his sartorial elegance either.

McBride got his fire going again. Fuel was no problem. His clearance of the building had revealed a lot more timber scrap. He went down into the sea and refilled his pot. When the water was boiling he dropped the crabs in. When they were a red colour, he judged them to be cooked and pulled them out with the aid of a stick. He then pulled the mussels from his pockets and dumped them in the water. They quickly opened. He gave them about six minutes, then pulled the pot off the fire, and left it to cool while he dressed the crabs. He had done this before, so he recognized the dead man's fingers and discarded them. Using stones he was able to crack the legs open to enjoy the flesh. He congratulated himself on his cooking skills. He was sure that the gulls would not have tasted so good, and he had left them to live another day.

He felt guilty sitting around after his meal, while there was work to be done. He went back into the building and found a brace and drill bit that would be useful. He had a plan. First, he had a worry that the barrels wouldn't be waterproof. He guessed that after maybe a century or more stored indoors, and empty, he guessed, the planks would have dried out and shrunk, the barrel hoops not clamping them anymore. If that had happened, then he could soak the barrels and eventually the wood, soaking up liquid, would expand and press tight. He found the barrel that had rolled off the floor this morning. It was empty, but the bung was in. He bowled the barrel out into the light, and prized out the cork bung with a screwdriver. Using the cooking bowl he poured seawater inside. The water spurted out between the planks and it was empty within seconds.

He pulled all the barrels out from beneath the flooring on the beach, and one or two extras from the building. He sauntered over to the freshwater pool, waded in to see how deep it was. Soon he was swimming, it was deeper than neck height.

He pulled all the empty barrels over to the pool, unprised all the bungs and sank all the barrels by holding them underwater until they filled. He would check how they were doing tomorrow.

Going back to the beach, he curled up before the fire, and was soon asleep.

Chapter 14

Jack Hopkins got to his office at eight in the morning, and the phone was ringing on his desk. He uttered some expletives, and dumped his briefcase on the top. He stretched across and lifted the phone, still standing, looking through the window down at the car park.

"Hopkins speaking."

"It's Stan Burrows here from Dulong. Harold Fox didn't report in last night. We sent a guy to his house, but it was all locked up, no sign of life. Even his servant wasn't in."

"Did Pepper report in?"

"Oh yes, no problem there."

"Did you ask Pepper if he knew where Fox was?"

"No, he reported in early. We didn't know Fox was missing then."

"Okay, break in to his house see if you can find any evidence about where he might have got to. I'll put a country wide alert out. Get back to me as soon as you've searched the house." He put the phone down, then lifted the handset again and got through to the super.

"Hopkins here, Sir. We've got a major problem. Fox has skipped. He didn't report in to Dulong station last night, and there's nobody at his house."

"Get a press conference organized for say, eleven this morning, here. I'll open up with a brief announcement, then you can answer questions about the case."

"Yes, Sir, the inquest is opening tomorrow, and we haven't found John McBride. I can't find anybody who has seen him for about four days. He's not been in to the exhibition, which is strange so the gallery owner says. Nobody has seen him near his apartment, we've questioned all his neighbors."

"Any un-identified bodies been reported? I don't want to be pessimistic, but you ought to check."

Hopkins agreed he would. He gave the job to a detective constable, and decided to motor to Dulong himself that afternoon. He couldn't go before because of the press conference. He went into the general office, pulled an able female detective constable off the reception desk, told her to phone the press and TV people with the news that a press conference would be held here at 11 am prompt. Subject: Disappearance of a witness on bail in the Dulong cult case.

He sat at his desk and drafted out a press release for distribution at the conference, and ran it through the photocopier. The press release had a photo of Harold Fox that had been taken at the police station when he was first apprehended. He looked smart in a collar and tie, hair neatly combed.

The press started coming in about ten to eleven, TV people first dragging equipment and setting up. There was a loud babble of voices, mostly people greeting each other. No excitement about the news; every day there was news; that was their job.

One of the constables distributed the press packs, as people queued up to get their copies. They sat around reading them. The super arrived, rapped on the lectern to quieten the noise and outlined the case, mentioned that two people were remanded on bail, one was now missing, his sergeant would answer any questions as far as possible. They would understand, as always, that some facts may not be divulged if it would hinder police work. The super recited all this as he had a hundred times before. He walked out of the door and Hopkins took his place.

"Good morning. First you will see from the press packs that we have a good likeness of the missing man, so I hope you will give the photo prominence. We think he is still in the country. He didn't have a passport."

A girl put up her hand. "He could have got himself a false passport."

Hopkins nodded. "It's possible. But we think it's unlikely that a false passport would have got through the sophisticated systems at airports."

"So you mean he might have got out by ship?"

"You're reading too much into my remarks."

A young man raised his arm. "How long has he been missing now?"

"He should have reported at five o'clock last night, but he didn't. His house is empty and locked up."

"So he could have been on the run for thirty-six hours. That must have been the last time you saw him?" He paused, having recalculated. "More than that, maybe forty hours."

Hopkins just nodded, not bothering to contest the facts.

"Even if he's not abroad, he could be anywhere in Australia. It's a big country."

Hopkins nodded again. "But not too many people, relatively for the amount of acreage. A lot of Australia is desert. If he's in the desert he's likely dead."

A lot of discussion took place between members of the press about what ports they had personal information. Hopkins picked up his notes from the lectern, rapped the edges to square them up, held them in his left hand. The TV guys were shutting down their cameras, looping up wiring, and packing boxes.

While Hopkins was packing to go over to Dulong, he switched on the TV in the corner of his office, to catch the midday news. The press conference got first item prominence, with the photograph of Harold Fox. Hopkins watched for a few moments then killed the set. On his way out to the car park he passed the switchboard and noted with satisfaction that three operators were busy with calls. The publicity was paying off.

In the car and entering the mountain passes, Hopkins imagined with gloom that he might spend the next six months commuting to Dulong. Perhaps he should hire an apartment, if there were such things out in the bush, and spend the next six months working over there trying to put the case to bed.

With the view coming up at last of the vast plain laid out in sunshine, his spirits rose, and he enjoyed the quiet drive over the flat land to the town of Dulong.

He parked outside the police house, locked the car and went in. The woman on the front desk shouted "Stan" in her hoarse voice and Stan poked his head through the inside door.

"Hi Stan, I thought I'd go check out Pepper, if you haven't asked him 'bout Fox. I take it he hasn't turned up?"

"No. I saw the news with Fox's photo. Maybe that will turn something up."

"Doubt it, but we were getting a lot of calls when I left the office. Anyway I'll go and see Pepper, and check out what he's got to say. I'd like to hear a bit more about their relationship. On my way back to Sydney I'll report back to you. If it's too late, then I'll speak to you on the phone tomorrow."

Hopkins got back in his car, and drove up the cult site. Very little seemed to have changed, perhaps some more clearance of the burned down building. He understood that Pepper lived in the first caravan, so he knocked on the door. The door was quickly opened by Pepper, who wore his dog collar over a t-shirt, and carried a pen in his hand.

Hopkins said, "Hello again, I'm here to talk with you about Harold Fox, maybe you know he's vanished, didn't report last night to Sergeant Burrows."

Pepper stood back from the caravan entrance and beckoned him in with the pen in his hand. "Come in. I was just writing a letter to my folk back home. That's in Utah." He led the way through to the lounge area, which contained a table with benches on two sides. On the table lay a writing pad, and a pack of envelopes in an open cardboard box.

Hopkins sat down on the opposite side of the table, and Pepper sat down in front of his letter. "How long have you known Fox? Were you close friends before you took this job?"

"I didn't know him at all. I answered an advertisement. One of our brothers pointed it out to me. Suggested it was good for me to go spread the word. That's how we've increased the number of Mormons now to about fifteen million. Fox said he needed somebody to run a religious cult. Previously he had run it himself until he became ill."

"But I understand he is well now."

"That is so, but he is quite old and wanted to retire. I got the job."

"I don't want to pry into your background. I've no doubt that the coroner will do that at the inquest. Where do you think Fox has gone?"

"I've got no idea. He didn't talk to me at all since we were arrested, and released on bail. I only knew he'd disappeared because I saw it on the television news at lunchtime. I was very surprised."

"You met a man called McBride who helped to rescue people during the fire?"

"I saw him talking to the fire chief, and one of the crew told me he was an English artist, some sort of soldier before that. That's all I know."

"Have you seen him since?"

Pepper looked at the table, didn't look Hopkins in the eye. "No." Hopkins thought that he was lying. It was the first time that he hadn't looked at Hopkins when he answered a question.

"You have seen him. When was it?" Hopkins spoke firmly.

Pepper fidgeted with his pen. "I haven't seen him. Where would I? I don't get away from the cult except when I've had to go to the police station. He hasn't been here since the fire."

Hopkins knew he wouldn't get any further unless he brought Pepper in. He hadn't been ready to do that. It might be a side issue, and maybe just a coincidence. But he had found that you must follow your nose when the case got tough, so he would take him back to Sydney, grill him there.

"I know you are lying when you say that you haven't seen McBride. Perhaps we can get you to tell me more back in Sydney. I am taking you in now. You will have to pass control here to one of your guiding angels. Make up your mind who, and we'll tell them."

Pepper looked scared, and for a moment Hopkins thought he was going to break down and confess. Suddenly, he seemed to make up his mind and draw strength from somewhere inside, perhaps in his faith, misguided though it may be.

Hopkins stood up, pulled a set of cuffs from his case. He clipped one cuff to Pepper's right hand, the other to his own left hand. "Okay, let's go and tell your deputy that you will be out of camp for a while."

They walked down the line of vans, and Pepper knocked on one of the doors. A man opened it, and, standing on the step, Pepper said, "I'm going to Sydney with the officer. Please take charge whilst I'm gone." As he turned away, Hopkins noticed tears in Pepper's eyes. What was that all about, he wondered. Dread or fear?

Looking back on the conversation on his way back to Dulong, he remembered that Pepper had looked him in the eye when he said *he hasn't been here since the fire.* That part was true, anyway.

He had Pepper in the back seat of the police car, with his handcuffs secured to the special rail provided for the purpose. There was no conversation between them.

Chapter 15

McBride woke up on the beach, and the sky was covered in a high cloud. No sun meant no fire, meant no hot food. Shit. It was day three today, or maybe day four.

With his limited diet he felt a perpetual hunger, but his figure was trimmer. More like it had been in his army days. He swore then and there that he would eat sensibly when and if he got back to civilization. He remembered about his barrel experiment, got up and ambled across to the fresh water pond. He wondered if the barrels had changed the taste of the water. He scooped up a handful and held the water in his mouth, washing it around to absorb any flavours. He got a background taste of rum. Ye Gods, distilling rum on a prison island?

He would go along the coast, hunting for food, and by the time he got back, the sun would be out and he could start his fire. At first the high cloud remained, but by the time he reached the cliffs, the cloud was denser, and odd spots of rain began to fall. By the time he reached the highest point of the cliff, the day was darkening, and the rain was heavy. It was cold, and the wind picked up. McBride began to shiver. He decided to make his way down the cliffs towards the lower ground and the shore. He clambered over the rocks and saw a gap that was big enough to get into, a sort of cave, he believed. It might be warm and would provide shelter from the rain which was now torrential. He climbed down, ducking his head, and he was inside, the area widening out, the headroom improving as the floor got lower.

He looked to the left, and what he saw made his heart beat faster.

Stretched out on a shelf of rock, like a bed with a boulder for a pillow lay a skeleton of a human, with all the bones complete as far as could be seen. The bones were bleached white, the skull with its huge eye craters seemed to be looking out to sea through the front aperture of the cave. And that must have been how he took his last breath, looking at the world, dreadfully ill maybe, or just starving to death, his organs closing down, one by one.

McBride imagined that he was probably the first person to have entered the cave since the man's death. Most likely he was an escaped prisoner who hid himself away from capture, but in vain. McBride sat himself on a shelf of rock on the opposite side of the cave, leaned back watching the rain lash down outside the gloomy cave. His eyelids drooped and the next thing he knew was opening his eyes, and seeing a vision on the opposite side of the cave. The human skull was bathed in an unholy light, a light that seemed to glow in the darkness of the cave. The skull was hanging in space. And then as McBride woke up properly he realized that it was a shaft of sunlight shining into the cave through the entrance, and falling exactly, precisely on the skull of the unknown man. McBride's blood was suddenly flowing back through his body, relief washing through him as he climbed to his feet, and eased himself through the cave entrance and into the soft warm air and sunshine.

He sauntered down through the rocks, arriving on the beach, paddling over to the old wreck, tearing at the mussels, filling his pockets with his breakfast.

He was in a hurry now. He had to make his voyage this very morning, and while, judging by the position of the sun, he hadn't slept for long in the cave, he needed to hurry. Immediately he got back to the campsite, filled his cooking pot with fresh water where it bubbled from the pond and tried to lift one of the barrels. It was too heavy. He managed to tip it on the side, and the water from inside gurgled as it escaped from the hole in the top. He pushed it to the edge of the pond, bowled it out on the bottom flange. It stood upright on dry land, and McBride realized it was not leaking. He sat down on the ground and watched it for half an hour. He walked round the barrel looking at the sandy soil. It was dry.

He spent the next two hours pulling out all the barrels, and rolling while full down to the beach, and left them by the floor which was soon to become a raft.

He ate a couple of apples while he was working. Then he went back to exploring the rest of the building. He still had bricks in there, and as he searched he disposed of them on the ground outside. The first prize he unearthed was a coil of stout rope. It hung at the back on a huge bracket. When he wrestled it down and examined it, he could see and feel that it was still in good condition. And why not, it had been stored in dry conditions. Amongst other treasures he unearthed were a couple of chisels and mallet, a half inch drill bit for the brace he had found the previous day, and unbelievably a couple of tarpaulins in the far corner, the last items he dragged out. He was ready to build the raft, though he reckoned it would take the rest of the day. So tomorrow, day five, would be when he got back to the mainland.

He got going with the saw and some nails; made a dagger board, which is a keel which the helmsman can lift by dragging it up through a close fitting slot in the boat, or in this case, a raft. If you don't have a keel, the boat won't dig into the water, and a side wind will push the boat, or raft sideways. If the keel doesn't lift, then you can't take the vessel into shallow water. His next job was to drill holes in the flanges of the barrels to attach the barrels to the raft by rope. He thought four barrels would give sufficient buoyancy. If it didn't work, he would add two more. He also drilled the boards of the raft to take the barrel ropes.

The mast needed a socket in which it would rest, and rope stays, three of them would hold the mast standing in the socket. A sail, in this case a lug sail made from one of the tarpaulin sheets, would be nailed to a length of wood which would itself be roped to the main mast. Ropes on each bottom corner would be held by the captain: McBride, so that he could adjust the sail, spilling wind or not, as necessary. He would be at the rear of the raft, because he would control the rudder which would to a slight degree steer the craft. The rudder, he realized. That was the last thing he needed. He fashioned it with planks, but made it so that it would hinge by putting a drilled hole and rope knots. A post was drilled into the boards. The rudder would turn on its axis.

The raft was ready for launching by four o'clock, but McBride was not going to risk starting a voyage at this late stage in the day, especially in a boat that had not been on a maiden voyage even. He decided that he would make everything ready for launching early the following morning.

The sun was still out. McBride assessed the time based on the sun's height. Early afternoon maybe two or even three o'clock. McBride was still not going to start his cruise today. Instead he lit the fire, stoked it up well, then damped it down so that it would burn whilst he foraged for his early dinner. He decided it would be another fish meal. The tide was well out.

He made the journey in only half an hour, and then he was on the sand and rocks, searching the pools. Luckily he caught a lobster that had been marooned by the falling tide. He carried it by the tail, its huge pincers snapping uselessly. At last he got back to the fire, stoked it up one handedly, put the cooking pot on the fire and waited until the water was hot. The lobster had by now tired itself out. It might have struggled for longer had it foretold its own fate. The pot was steaming now, and McBride dropped the lobster in. It struggled briefly before giving itself up.

McBride went over to the pool and dug a few potatoes for his last meal on the island. Eating mussels, lobster and potatoes as the sun dropped towards the horizon, made him sentimental towards the island. He lay down by the remains of the fire, and looked towards his finished boat. The waves were lapping on the prow, which was only obvious by the rudder being at the other end. The mast stood proudly, the sprit on the deck, with a bundle of tarpaulin ready to be hoisted aloft. Although the raft was nothing much to look at, McBride thought it well constructed and undoubtedly able to sail the twelve miles to the mainland, with McBride himself on board and at the helm.

Mc Bride spent a long and disturbed night. The wind got up, and he was worried that a bad storm might ruin his chances of sailing the next day. But when he finally opened his eyes when the sun rose, it was to see a clear blue sky, and the sea was fairly smooth. But the beach was in the lee of the island, and the wind invariably a westerly. He ate the last two of his apples and stood up.

The tide was at its highest as McBride had worked out it would be. The water was again lapping at the raft. He rolled up his trousers and waded into the sea. Last night he had used the spare two barrels in the center of the raft's width, so that a slight pull on the front of the raft would start the barrels rolling, and the raft plunging into the water. When he was up to his knees, the raft had bobbed clear, and was floating. He clambered aboard, and even with his weight, it was still floating. The boarding was just above the waterline, though small waves flooded across the wooden surface. That didn't worry McBride, you always got wet on a raft, better than the alternative: swimming or drowning.

He pulled up the mainsail, and tied off the rope with a slipknot so that it could easily be dropped in storm conditions. The test came when they came out from the lee of the island. The raft shot forward, and for McBride it was like being in shower as the spray from the raft's leading edge hit him full face. He spilled some wind out of the sail, and the raft reduced speed. Much better. For a start he could see where they were heading. He aimed to take a diagonal course towards the mainland; that was where the concentration of light was after dark. It must be Melbourne, he reckoned.

He was now traveling comfortably over the sea now, except when a wave overtook the raft, and McBride was momentarily sitting in an inch or three of water. And it was cold. But that didn't happen very often. But other exciting things required some alertness. For example, the rocks, jutting like tiny islands. He had to keep all his wits about him. To be shipwrecked was not on his agenda.

Almost as he thought this, the water became calmer, and he realized he was close to the mainland and heading for a beach which would be perfect. McBride adjusted the sail to reduce speed, pulled at the rudder to direct the raft centrally on the sloping sand. As the raft approached the sand, McBride was aware that they were approaching too fast. He slipped the knot and the sail tumbled down. The raft came on relentlessly, and McBride leaned forward, pulling up the dagger keel board just in time, and the raft barrels skidded on the sand, the raft suddenly stopped, McBride was projected off the raft. And landed on fairly dry sand above the waterline. One barrel broke free and rolled a few feet further ashore. He was back on the Australian mainland. Looking ahead he could see vehicles moving along the coast road.

Cautiously, he stood up. No pain and seemingly no broken bones. From his standing position, he could see that there were only a few grass covered dunes separating him from the road edge. He walked slowly up and over the dunes, aware that he must look like a filthy hobo, his clothes creased and wet, dirty from his search of the disused building, and from sleeping on the beach. If he tried to thumb a lift, would anyone stop for him? There was only one way to find out.

He crossed the road when it was clear of traffic. The next vehicle in his direction was an old pick-up truck driven by a white haired guy leaning the elbow of his right arm on the open window. He saw McBride when he was a way off, and began to slow up. He stopped directly beside him. The left window was down too.

"You going to Melbourne? Hop in."

"That's very kind. Sorry my clothes are a bit wet. Hope I don't spoil your truck."

"Ain't much left to spoil. You bin swimming? Fell off a boat?"

"Got marooned on an island by someone that didn't like me. Made a raft and sailed back. Just landed on the beach down there. Been sleeping and working in my clothes, so I'm not looking good."

"You're a lucky young man. You sailed in from further west?"

McBride nodded. "How did you guess? Oh, the prevailing wind you mean."

"No, not only that. If you'd have sailed another three miles or so, I wouldn't be talking to yer now. It's the rips, you see. Killed our old prime minister, what, sixty years ago. Went for a swim and never came back out again." He nodded. "The rips."

"What do you mean, rips?"

"The rip tides. Underwater currents going this way and that. Few miles along the coast. Taken twelve hundred boats, they have. All gone to the bottom." He concentrated on overtaking a tractor. "Including our prime minister."

McBride said, "Someone told me I had the luck of the Irish."

"I'd have put you down as a pom," said the old man, peering at him as though he could tell an English man from an Irish man.

"I'm English, you're right there, but my ancestors were Irish. Name is McBride."

"That's Irish, right enough."

Chapter 16

They drove along in amiable silence, then the old man said, "Where can I drop you off, Mr. McBride?" The traffic was building up as they entered the suburbs of Melbourne. McBride had already spotted the road to the marina, where he had begun the fateful journey.

"Anywhere will do, I can get a cab. I don't want to get you snarled up in the city center traffic."

"That's no problem. I like it in Melbourne. Let me be the judge."

"Well, I was booked in at the downtown Marriott."

"I know where that is. You don't want them to rip you off. Tell them you came here with Jonty Smithers. You got that?"

Several minutes later Jonty pulled the old truck up at the front of the hotel. He held out his hand to McBride. He shook it. "Thank you very much. There wouldn't be many that would pick up someone just out of the sea." The old man smiled, and put the truck into gear, and pulled away in a cloud of grey smoke.

The doorman opened the glass door. "Welcome to the Marriott, Sir. Excuse me for asking but was that Jonty Smithers dropped you off?"

"You know him." McBride was surprised.

"Of course. Richest man in Melbourne, but he doesn't act like it. Owns all the land round the city center."

McBride went over to the reception desk. A smart middle aged man smiled and wished him a good day.

"I booked in four days or even five days ago, and left my luggage, but I was called away somewhat urgently. Now I'm back I wonder if you have a room for me?"

"Of course, Sir. The name is?"

"McBride, John McBride."

The man looked at his computer screen.

"When you booked in last time, the hotel was no way full. There will be no charge for that night, Sir. How long will you be staying this time?"

"Just tonight, then I go back to Sydney. But I'll be back for a longer stay in a week or two."

When he got to his room, McBride's only thought was to have a very long shower and a change of clothes. But he had to make a phone call urgently. His cell phone was missing, stolen he suspected, by Harold Fox. He used the room phone.

When he was connected to the police he asked to speak to Sergeant Jack Hopkins. After a few moments, Hopkins came on the line.

"Who is it?"

"John McBride, I just got back, so I'm reporting in. I'm in Melbourne, I haven't been back to my Sydney address yet. I suppose I've missed the inquest?"

"No you haven't. It's been put back until Monday."

"I'm a little muddled with the date. Is today Thursday?"

"God, man, are you on drugs?"

"No. I'm flying back to Sydney tomorrow morning. Shall I call in at your office when I get there?"

"If you would. I'm at the office all day." He didn't seem very friendly thought McBride as he stripped his dirty clothing off and dumped the lot into the waste bin.

A long shower and a change of clothing gave him a feeling of belonging again to the human race, and a saunter along the street to an Italian restaurant cheered him up no end. When he came out an hour and a half later he felt no hunger for the first time in four days. He went straight back to the hotel and into his bed at only four thirty in the afternoon. He slept until 6 am the following day.

He was first into the breakfast room, having paid his bill, and at seven thirty was in a cab to the airport. He bought a ticket for the first flight to Sydney.

It was ten thirty when McBride walked into the Sydney police station. Jack Hopkins met him in the entrance hall and took him up to the office.

When they were seated, Hopkins said, "We were looking for you, we did know you'd gone missing. Tell me the story." So McBride gave a brief rundown how he thought he was meeting with the gallery owner in Melbourne where the next exhibition was scheduled. In fact he had never met Fox before, but when he got down to Fox's boat his suspicions were aroused by the name on the boat. He also found out, at the moment of being abandoned on the island that Pepper had also been on the boat.

Hopkins interrupted. "I knew Pepper was lying when he told me he hadn't seen you since the fire. I'm sorry, please go on."

McBride told him how he vowed that he would get back on the mainland in seven days. In fact it was only four, or maybe five days.

"You're not looking bad for being marooned, tanned and you look as if you lost some weight."

McBride grinned. "A lot of physical effort, and not a lot to eat, besides seafood, you know, lobster and so on." He laughed.

Hopkins said, "What about caviar?" McBride shook his head. "No rich food."

"Seriously, did you know that Fox has jumped bail? We haven't found him yet, but he hasn't got a passport."

"What about Pepper?"

"We'd still got him reporting every day to the police station in Dulong. But yesterday I pulled him in, and currently he's in the cells here. We've just been questioning him last night. He spilled quite a bit about kidnapping you and abandoning you on an island. He says that Fox made him help, under duress. Well he would. He's a bit of an oddball. Can't say I like him.

"So you see, we were on the case, and if you hadn't phoned me, I would have been in Melbourne, down in the marina, questioning the harbour master, finding out the time that Fox's boat went out and came back again. They were bound to have it logged down somewhere. These sea-farers are like that, big on record keeping. Then I would have done some calculations, using charts and so on, to work out which island you could have been on. That could have saved you some trouble. In the end you saved me some."

"That's what I think as well." He stood up, and put out his hand. "I'll see you at the inquest."

"Not for long, it's bound to be adjourned because of Fox's absence."

"I'd like to get my hands on Fox, he's a nasty piece of work. If you haven't found him by the end of the inquest, I'll go and find him myself." And he walked downstairs and out of the police station.

It had been a while since McBride had visited his exhibition and he thought it politic to show his face. So rather than go back to his apartment, he walked down to the gallery. The owner was standing in the main room, and he smiled broadly when he saw McBride, and said, "Welcome stranger. I nearly sent a search party out for you."

McBride took his hand. "I wish you had. First you would have needed a boat."

He looked puzzled and McBride elaborated.

"Good God, you could have died, and not been discovered for years."

"Not John McBride. I was in the SAS Regiment. They really teach you to look after yourself. I was quite worried not coming in to the gallery regularly. When have I promised to do a demo painting?"

"Next week on the Friday afternoon. I hope you won't miss it."

"Not a chance."

Chapter 17

The next morning John McBride had an overwhelming urge to do some painting. It had seemed like weeks since he had picked up his brushes, but it was actually more like at best a couple of weeks. He gathered up his painting gear, and went off straight after breakfast. It was an unsurprisingly nice day, sunny. He was singing a tune under his breath as he walked along the street, easel folded up under one arm, and a board under the other. No seat, because he always stood to paint, claiming that it ensured he painted the right horizon line without having to correct for this.

It was quite a long walk until he got near the waterfront, with a view of the iconic bridge, and plenty of boats. This was the sort of subject that McBride really liked, and he had searched out the scene before he was kidnapped, and a view he had vowed to paint. Now, here he was. He spent some time searching for just the right composition, because composition was the most important factor of any image.

The position of the bridge across the painting was important. It had to feature importantly, yet not block out the sky. In the golden position was to be a yacht sailing into the painting, towards the bridge. The golden position was so-called by the seventeenth and eighteenth painters, and was approximately a third of the way across a painting, and about one third of the way up. McBride had found this out from his own experimentation, and only much later found that the old masters had discovered the square shape was too constricting, and so came up with the 'four/three' shape. This was so *right* that the first movies had adopted the shape, and also television sets. Now of course most media has moved to 1:1.69 horizontal ratio, known initially as *cinemascope*. McBride generally painted large paintings in A3, which is basically 4 x 3 ratio, and this was the size he had fastened with tape to his board, a paper on each side so that if he made a serious error he would reluctantly start again. This happened very rarely now he had over fifteen years' experience. Now it was mainly so that he could do two paintings at least on any outing.

He set up his easel, which was a tripod with a box on top, a drawer to keep his paints, water, brushes, and a frame above this to carry the board at an adjustable angle, and at a height so that he could stand to paint. The legs were individually adjustable in height, so that the painting paper could always be kept horizontal. Without that happening, it could result in skewed paintings which could never be corrected.

He stood behind the easel, and the view was perfect, allowing him to transfer the view on to paper size for size. It was not only the easiest way, but it allowed him to concentrate on colour and tonal values. And also deliberate alterations from true life, slight changes that would improve even more the composition. McBride always painted standing up, for two reasons: it meant that he didn't have to carry a seat around with him. He had enough baggage with his easel and drawing board. Secondly by standing he was painting at the normal eye level, or horizon line. Sitting down brought the horizon line up, and it made the image wrong to the viewer, most of whom wouldn't know the reason, but discard the painting as 'not very good' without being able to say why.

He worked with diligence to accurately sketch the scene in pencil until he was satisfied with the results. Finally he pulled the palette from the drawer in front of him. Hearing a cough from behind, he turned to see a number of spectators. He smiled at them all, and then saw Jack, the detective, amongst the crowd.

"Hello, there! No detecting to be done today?"

"I'm on late shift. I'm watching you in my own time. I hope there's no charge." Whilst Jack had been speaking, people were moving to allow him to get near McBride.

"You've come at the right time, now is when I paint." He gestured with his palette and grabbed the first tube of paint. He filled six of the paint holders along the top with his six basic colours.

"I only work with six basic colours. From these, I can mix most of the others, and the whole painting will hold together, colour-wise. If you were to take one of these children's paint boxes that contain about twenty-four or even thirty blocks of paint and use them on a painting it would turn out just like the paint box, a riot of colour hiding the scene." Whilst he was talking he had continued squeezing his six colours into the pans. Now he poured out a bottle of water into an expandable plastic jar that looked a little like a concertina. He hung the bottle on a convenient hook on the side of his easel. Then he mixed a blob of cobalt blue into water he had put into the mixing pan on the palette with a large brush. He mixed the paint thoroughly, adding a very small dab of red, to take the edge off the colour. "If I added more red, it will give me a lovely grey that I can use for the shadows"

"This is the biggest brush I use, a number twenty. Made of sable hair like all my brushes. It holds water well, and is soft, and shapes well when it is wet."

He filled the brush, and swept it quickly across the top of the paper. It left an inch wide stripe of colour, and the angle of the board allowed a bead of liquid along the bottom edge of the colour. He quickly dipped the brush into the clean water and stirred the brush in the paint. Quickly he brushed across the paper, picking up the surplus paint that was already there, so that it was now a band that was twice as wide but there was no break visible. By the time McBride had repeated the action a further three times, Jack could see that the sky was gradually getting a lighter blue as it moved down to the horizon. Just as it should, and as it was in the scene in front of him.

McBride worked fast and without stopping until he had blocked in all the sky. Miraculously that coincided with the last of the paint McBride had prepared. Waste not, want not. Jack said to McBride, "I'm on my way to lunch. Do you fancy joining me?"

"I would love to, but once I've started on a painting, I continue until it's finished. For one thing the weather changes, and the time changes."

"What's the time got to do with it?" said Jack.

"The position of the sun," McBride told him without stopping. "I should have it finished in about an hour. Is that any good?"

"Don't rush. I'll hang about. I'm not on duty until six this evening. You certainly knock out a painting quickly, don't you?"

McBride grinned.

"Twenty years learning how to do it first. Water colour is meant to be a fast medium. If you paint painstakingly instead of swiftly, nobody would buy the results."

Whilst he was talking to Jack, McBride's hands were working quickly, mixing more paint, applying it fast and surely, the bridge now taking shape on the paper.

"The trick is to give the impression of adding detail, but really only giving the eye enough for the mind to complete the picture itself. If it was complete in every tiny detail, your mind, and everyone else's mind would quickly lose interest. That is the over-riding secret of painting. It applies even more in abstract art. Only that is a step too far for some people, thank God."

Jack looked puzzled. "Why do you say 'thank God?'

"Because I prefer this sort of painting, and it earns me a pretty good living."

All the time he was talking and holding a conversation, he was still painting. Now he was painting the yacht which was the subject. But the yacht was actually moored in the harbour, sails stowed, a dinghy afloat and moored to the stern. The owner was obviously aboard, perhaps having elevenses. But McBride knew his yachts. As he would, having a father who sailed competitions as a member of the Yorkshire Yacht Club at Bridlington. He was allowed to crew with his dad every weekend, certainly on Sundays. On Saturday it depended whether he was needed at the St Peter's school for a rugger match.

And so McBride depicted the yacht at anchor as fully rigged, and moving under sail, slightly at an angle from the wind on the beam, the mainsail and jib aloft, pennant fluttering on top of the mast, figures on deck holding ropes, one at the helm in yellow waterproofs. The mainsail had the reefing ties loose as the sail was unreefed. McBride had mixed cobalt and red to give shadow grey, and had put shadows on the sails, using a small brush to blend the shadows into the stark whiteness where the sun shone on them.

The whiteness came from the paper itself. But McBride made sure that the boat itself was the main feature by giving depth to the hull's shadows, rigging and rails. He put the correct numbers on the sails, copied from the hull of the boat itself. He painted bow waves, and a roughish wake, with much darkness in the shadows between the waves. He then turned to the distant shore seen below the bridge itself, greenish in the distance, some light green, some very deep green, almost dark grey. He used a brush in either hand, one loaded with light green, one the dark. He wielded the brushes so that the paint ran slightly into the other. Finally he finished with some shore items, lamp posts, a large tree. He painted traffic crossing the bridge as smudges, still identifiable though.

Finally, he loaded his biggest brush with white gouache paint which is a water soluble opaque paint. He laid the brush sideways, so that he was swiping the brush lightly across the paper, only contacting the projecting grain of the paper. He did this across the water towards the bridge. The result was small white topped waves, where a gust of wind might have passed. It completed the painting. Giving it a cursory glance, he removed the painting from the easel.

"The painting is complete," he announced to the onlookers with a smile. "And I am going to lunch."

Walking down the street with Jack on the way to their lunch, Jack carrying McBride's

easel folded into its suitcase appearance, and McBride himself with the painting on its board tucked under his arm, the police inspector said, "How did you get involved in this painting lark? Did you go to art school when you left secondary school?"

McBride smiled. "Hardly. I was destined for the

army. I won a place at Sandhurst with the aim of joining the SAS Regiment. I was a very gung ho sort of boy, member of the school cadet force. We use to have a camp every summer out in the dales. That was the reason I joined actually." He grinned. "I achieved what I wanted, got a commission in the SAS. My God, the training was hard once I got into the regiment. And then we were posted to Iraq, once it was decided to go to war. We were actually parachuted in before the first assault, to recce the way. I spent a lot of time in the desert, even though it wasn't a long war. It's a funny thing about being in the army. You spend a lot of time sitting about, and then short intense periods of action. In the times that there was very little happening, a very good friend and comrade used to paint in water colour, which of course is the ideal medium for people on the move. I used to watch him painting, and I thought: I would like to do that. I asked him if he would teach me the rudiments, and he did. Over a period of the next twelve months. First he told me the correct tackle to buy, the right paper to use, the professional paints. He taught me techniques. My first attempts were abysmal, and I nearly gave up. I went back to the art shop, and bought some videos by well known painters. The videos showed painters actually producing work from beginning to end. And at last I began to produce acceptable work. When I was on leave I often attended classes by the same favorite artists. I really worked at it, you might say.

"I always painted from life, especially scenes of townscapes, villages and so on. The Yorkshire Dales are not far from the town I live in, Skipton. On the doorstep, really. I still hadn't sold a painting, but my paintings were getting good. One day I was painting in the dales. There was a group of people watching me, three or four. That always happens. I know some people are put off their stride by this, but it doesn't faze me. In fact I sometimes give a running commentary about what I am doing, every step of the way completing a painting. I actually give demonstrations these days in the galleries I exhibit in."

They crossed the street, and turned a corner, Jack leading the way to a restaurant he knew. McBride carried on: "I was painting in the dales this particular day, and a voice next to me said: 'You are a good painter, you have a gift not given to many. I own a few galleries and supply even more. I could sell all the paintings you can do.' I looked at him, and he looked sincere. So I told him that I lived a short distance away and if he came back with me, I had about forty paintings there. He could take them, and I would phone him next time I was home on leave, and see how many if any he had sold."

They had arrived at the door of the restaurant. "I think you should like this place, John," the policeman said, "it's considered Australian in style."

The name above the door was *Blue Fish*. Inside the place was heaving, but it transpired Jack had a table reserved. They were shown to their places and left with two lunch menus. Jack said, "I hope you like fish, because there is little else."

"You know I do, from the castaway experience I had. My favorite is oysters, fresh ones."

"I thought all you poms ate fried fish and chips."

McBride looked up from the menu. "A lot of us do, some of the time. It's a long time since all of us did it all of the time. It started to as a dish that was cheap, sold as a take-away, around the mid-nineteenth century, and brought to England by German Jews, but don't quote me on that."

Jack put down his menu. "I always have the same meal every time I come here. Which is, guess what…? fish and chips. And every time I vow I'll try something else. But I don't."

McBride said, "I'll have the seafood feast, which includes oysters, so that's great."

When they had given their orders to the waiter, Jack said, "Going back to your story about becoming an artist, what had your agent got to say when you phoned him when you next came on leave?"

"He'd sold all forty paintings, and could he have some more? When I got back to the regiment I gave my notice, and became a professional artist."

"And never regretted it?" said Jack.

"I wouldn't say that. I love painting, but there are times that I miss the thrills of army life, the adventures. That is why I sometimes get involved in adventures, I guess."

Chapter 18

The Coroner's Court was wood paneled and smelled of furniture wax with an overtone of lemon air freshener. The background hum of an air conditioning unit could be heard very faintly.

The Coroner in a charcoal suit and red tie entered and sat at the desk on the raised platform. On one side of the room was a witness box, and the end of the room opposite the coroner was reserved for the public in a railed off area, with a small press compound. Opposite the witness box was the seating area for officials.

The coroner tapped his gavel very quietly on his desk, and began to read from a bound document in front of him. He announced the opening of the inquest on the death of thirteen women in a fire at the residential building named the Children of Messiah in Dulong, New South Wales on September 3rd.

John McBride was sitting in the public area, but knew he was being called as a witness this very morning. The coroner's voice droned on as he outlined the case. A few flies buzzed in the calm of the room. And then the coroner was calling the first witness, John McBride. He got up and walked into the witness box. He was asked for his full name and occupation.

The coroner said, "You were at the property of the Children of Messiah when it caught fire. Would you tell us, firstly why you were there at that time, and what you saw."

"I must explain that I had previously met a member of the cult, a woman in her twenties called Lucy, who attended an art exhibition I was holding at the Western Gallery in Sydney. She was in her mid-twenties I would estimate, and was in the company of a man and woman who I assumed at first were her parents. She was leaving the gallery and came over to say that she liked my artwork, and held out her hand to shake mine. I saw that she was trying to pass a note to me under cover of the handshake. This she did, and when I read the note later, it revealed that she wanted me to phone her on a cell phone she had recently obtained. She was painfully thin, and when I phoned her she revealed that she was very hungry." McBride paused and took a sip of water from the glass in front of him. "It appeared from the conversation

that she had to do things she didn't want to in order to get fed. She didn't enlarge on that.

"I thought in view of that meeting with Lucy, I would investigate the cult. I approached in daylight initially, but was met by a man with a rifle who threatened me.

"I went back on the night of the fire, covertly going round the plot the building is on, and approached the building from the rear. The car park at the back was occupied by a lot of cars and trucks with men in them. The back door opened, and names were shouted, and men went inside as others came out. I had the impression that it was being operated as a brothel. A storm had been brewing up for some time, with lightning over the mountains. Then the building was struck at the end away from me. I saw it strike the peak of the roof, and the tiles caught fire. They were falling from the building and igniting the bushes beside the building. The fire ran along the roof at quite a speed. I rushed up to the building to a door midway along, calling to other men to help. Only one of them accompanied me.

"We found that the bedrooms were locked, so we smashed the doors with our feet. This slowed up our rescue attempts, and when Reverend Pepper came along the corridor I asked him if he had the keys to the bedrooms. At this stage he was coughing as the smoke was entering the corridor, and he collapsed on the floor. I put my hand in his pockets and pulled out a bunch of keys. I found a key that fitted the bedroom doors, and the rescue went faster. Eventually we were overcome by smoke, and firemen had arrived, who carried on, and we were led outside.

"We continued to help rescued people who were lying on the grass. Ambulances arrived and we continued to help. Eventually the fire was put out, but it was dawn when this happened. I was sitting by the fence talking to the fire chief, when a fireman came up and told the chief he had found some graves in the orchard. We went to look, and there were six graves in a row, The last grave in the row was marked 'Lucy', written on a stick with black marker pen. I was very upset."

The coroner spoke. "Have you seen Mr. Pepper since?"

"I have seen him here this morning, although I haven't spoken to him."

"Have you seen him before this morning but after the night of the fire?"

"Yes, Sir. I was kidnapped on the day following the fire. I received a phone call purporting to be from a gallery owner in Melbourne, where I am giving an exhibition next month. My agent arranged the details, but I haven't met the man myself. It was arranged that I would visit Melbourne where the man would pick me up at the airport and drive me to the marina, where he had a boat. We would have some refreshments, and finalize details of the show. That didn't seem strange, so I agreed."

"Apparently who you met was in fact Mr. Harold Fox, who owned the cult?"

"Yes, Sir, I know that now. I had never met Mr. Fox before, although I had heard of him. There was also another man on the boat, below deck. I heard movements from the cabin, and I assumed he was in the galley preparing nibbles, which were served with alcoholic drinks."

"Go on," said the coroner.

"I realized when my drink was finished that I'd been given what I believe is called a spiked drink, because I quickly lost consciousness. When I regained consciousness, I was being carried by two men on to the beach of an island. Although I was conscious I could not move, although I could see. I went to sleep for some hours and when I woke, I was able to stand and move about. The effects of the drug had worn off."

The coroner held his glasses in his hand. "Did you recognize either of your captors at this time?"

"I saw that one of the men was Mr. Pepper. He must have been below deck when we were in the marina. The other man, now that I have seen photographs, was Harold Fox."

There was a gasp of surprise from the public seats, and the press were writing quickly in notebooks. Pepper had a very red face, and was staring at his knees.

The coroner looked at his watch and then declared an adjournment for early lunch. The court would resume at 1 pm.

Members of the public made a dash for the door, jostling one another in an attempt to be out first. The press filed out of their compound and McBride felt someone tap on his shoulder. He turned to see a young man smiling, and recognized John Hoskin the reporter from the *Daily Herald.*

"Hello, I didn't think you were on the news reporting staff."

Hoskin grinned. "Dead man's shoes. Well not really, the man I'm replacing has just retired. And I hope he won't die for a long time. I was wondering if I could buy you lunch?"

"So that you could get a story? Sure, why not." They walked out of the building side by side. The sun blinded them both after the gloom of the court, and McBride pulled a pair of dark glasses out of his top pocket.

"Sydney folk are more accustomed to the sun," Hoskin said, nodding at the sunglasses. Shows that you are a pom."

"Better than being mistaken for an Aussie," McBride said. "Watch your language if you want a story from me." Hoskins led the way down a narrow side street, and into a small Italian café, that made no attempt to look stylish, but the row of tables outside were all filled.

Inside it looked slightly scruffy, the tables were close together to make the most of the space available. There was a queue in front of a refrigerated counter.

Hoskin turned to McBride. "Go grab a table, and wait there. I'll order here and join you. Get cutlery from there on the way." He pointed to a shelf.

McBride found a small two seat table in the corner of the room, sat down and waited. The cutlery came wrapped in paper napkins and he put one set in front of each seat. Within minutes, Hoskins arrived and sat down. He had two side plates with him. Each contained green and black olives, and a hunk of bread with a pat of butter.

He said, "There's pasta on its way. It's sea food tagliatelle with tomato sauce. I recommend it."

"A diet of seafood is what I lived on last week, you can quote me," McBride said.

"Sorry, I didn't think."

"No need. I like sea food, honestly." With that, an overweight Italian brought two dishes of pasta, dumped them on the table, left the bill, and dashed off. It seemed to McBride that the husband was the cook, and the wife, front of house, and in charge of drinks.

Hoskins remembered something, and put both hands in his jacket pockets and came out with two bottles of Peroni beer. The caps had been removed. "Sorry about that," he said.

"Can I ask you questions as we eat?" asked Hoskins, he had brought a notebook and pen from his pocket and laid them on the table. "We don't have a lot of time before the court starts again. So which island where you marooned on?"

"I don't know, there were no signs on it." He smirked at Hoskins. "It was about twelve miles off the coast, a bit west of Melbourne. On the island was a big building. Not the remains of a mansion, more a government type building, with the front ripped off. Signs of horticulture, for example a small apple orchard, potatoes, and a freshwater pond. It was fed by a spring. The water might have come from the mainland mountains."

Hoskins interrupted. "Could have been an old prison settlement. Victoria State pride themselves on not being convicts shipped over from Britain, but they needed to put their own bad boys somewhere. That was in the nineteenth century, but they are more humane now."

"So I spent what time I wasn't hunting for food in building a raft. The easiest craft to build, you know. Fortunately there was rubble from the building, including timber, and old barrels would you believe."

"What did you do with the raft when you landed back here?"

"Left it lying on the beach, and hoofed it up to the coast road. Tell you what, the guy in an old truck I hitched was called Smithers. Apparently a wealthy soul, so I was told when he dropped me off at the hotel."

"Gosh, Smithers. A legend in his own lifetime." Hoskins seemed as truly impressed as every other Australian who knew about his meeting. "Tell you what, do me a sketch of the raft. I'll send our Melbourne man to look for it and photograph it."

So McBride sketched in Hoskins' notebook a likeness of the raft. "There were some sand dunes with grass on between the sandy beach and the road."

He asked some further questions about the island, the weather, and commented upon McBride's healthy tan. "Well, it didn't rain much while I was there. I think I was four days marooned, although it could have been five. Time really flies when you're busy trying to get back to civilization. Soon as I'd got the raft ready, I was out of there. Hey, here's something – while I was there a boat came past with two people in it, a small cruiser. They saw me and I waved like mad, waving my shirt." He laughed. "They waved back, and carried on. Are all Aussies that thick?" Hoskins lifted his notebook as though to hit him, but he was smiling. "They thought: must be some pom. Leave him."

Chapter 19

At one o'clock, John McBride was again standing in the witness box on his own volition, because that is where he was when the lunch recess had been called. At one minute past one precisely, the coroner came into the court and took his place at the desk. He stood and looked around the room.

"I think that we have finished with your evidence unless you are recalled later, Mr. McBride You are free to leave, or can take a seat in the public section."

McBride moved out of the witness box, and sat down in the public seating area. The coroner called up witnesses who were members of the sect, girls who had been rescued from the fire. He asked them to step into the witness box two at a time. McBride assumed that it was to make them feel more comfortable to have a colleague with them.

He spoke to the first two. "During your time living in the residence known as Children of Messiah, have you always been locked in your bedrooms, I mean every bedtime?"

"Yes, always. At nine o'clock until six o'clock in the morning. We start work at six thirty. Farm work, either with the sheep and cows, or working in the gardens."

The elder one, or that was what she seemed, answered. The other girl just gazed around her.

"Do you have any idea why you were locked up?"

"No."

"On the night of the fire, did you try to get out of the windows?"

"No, the windows don't open. And the glass is too hard to break, and the panes are too small to get through."

"How did you try to protect yourself against the fire?"

"I laid under the bed and prayed to my Guarding Angel to save me. She didn't come for me though."

The coroner looked puzzled. "Your angel from heaven, you mean?"

"No our Guarding Angel that lives further down the corridor." The coroner decided to let that pass for the moment. There were whispered comments between the public in the seating area.

The coroner continued to question all the girls, but got no further information. They appeared not to know very much as to why they were locked in, or about the people who ostensibly looked after them. Most of them had been with the cult since they were children of three or four. None of them could remember where they had been before that. They did not have parents in the cult, only guarding angels, both men and women. They were in their mid-twenties, yet they seemed to accept their position in the group, and were expected to work seven days a week in the farm. The food they produced was consumed by them, and also sold in Dulong.

When all twelve of the unharmed women had been cross-examined with no further information coming to light, the coroner addressed them. "Thank you for attending today, and I am now dismissing you to return to your…er…cult."

A man and a woman both looking as though they were in their early sixties, were organizing the young women to move off.

The coroner said, "Excuse me, are you two the young women's 'guarding angels'?"

The man looked up, and said, "Yes, we are."

If the young ladies will just sit down and wait, would both of you…angels like to step into the witness box? I won't keep you long."

Sounds of shuffling as the previous witnesses sat down, and the angels stepped into the box. The coroner eyed them with interest.

"How long have you two been "guarding angels" could you tell me?"

They looked at one another and the man said, "About twenty, or twenty-two, years, give or take."

"Just let me ask you this – why 'guarding angels'? Surely the description should be guardian angels?"

The man cleared his throat. "It was, but when the children were babies, they couldn't pronounce the word *guardian,* and so ever since we have been *guarding.* And in a way that is what we do, guard them through life. They were orphans, you see."

"And they are still here nearly into their thirties. How odd."

The woman spoke. "It is not odd, we look after them, why would they want to leave?"

"I've no time to argue the point with you. Why do you lock them up?'

The man said, "The building is out in the country a long way from civilization. If they strayed they could meet with danger."

For a long time, the coroner looked at the couple without saying anything. Then he said, "You are free to leave. Take your ladies with you." He began tidying his desk, moving files and restacking them. He was clearly disturbed, and McBride noticed that, for one.

Eventually, after the ladies had trouped out following their guardian angels, the coroner looked up, and looked for a long while at Pepper, who dropped his eyes, and appeared to squirm.

The coroner rapped his gavel on the desk to suppress the fidget of the public, and said, "Mr. Pepper, will you please step into the witness box."

Pepper, with apparent reluctance, stood up and moved into the box.

"You are Christopher Pepper, in charge of the Children of Messiah sect in Dulong?"

"Yes, Sir."

"Who appointed you?"

"Harold Fox. He advertised for a spiritual leader for the sect. I applied for the post, when a colleague pointed it out to me. He told me that it was a chance to spread the word."

"What word would this be?"

"I am a Mormon, Sir. Spreading the word is what we do. There are now over fifteen million Mormons worldwide, although the majority are in the United States."

"Is Mr. Fox aware that you are a Mormon?"

"Yes, Sir."

"But he is not a Mormon himself?"

"No, but he thinks I am capable of looking after the cult. I am still a Christian, Sir."

"Let me change the subject." The coroner looked down at his notes. "You heard Mr. McBride's evidence this morning. Is it true that you aided Mr. Harold Fox in kidnapping Mr. McBride?"

"Mr. Fox asked me if I would help crew his motor launch. He said that he was inviting a guest aboard for drinks, and would I work in the galley. I didn't see the guest until we started out to sea. In fact I thought he was only entertaining in the marina, and I was surprised when he started the engines, and had me help to undo the lines. Apparently Mr. McBride was ill at that time. I could see that he was unconscious. I helped to carry him ashore onto an island. When we returned to the marina, Mr. Fox drove me back to Dulong, and told me not to discuss what had taken place."

"Does Mr. Fox ask you to do illegal things often?"

"No, Sir. In fact I don't often see him, except when he collects the rent."

"The rent?" The coroner seemed surprised. "He charges the cult rent for the property. Is that what you mean?"

"I believe it is his only income, Sir."

"And he lives in a big house with servants and drives an expensive car, I believe. What rent does he charge?"

"Ten thousand dollars a month, Australian," said Pepper after a long pause.

The coroner cleared his throat. "And how do you manage to pay this rent. Where do you get the money from?"

Pepper paused for a long moment. Then: "Well, we sell farm produce in Dulong."

"I thought maybe incorrectly, that the farm was merely to make you self-sufficient?"

"Yes, but there is some produce left over."

"Ten thousand dollars' worth every month?"

"No, Sir"

"Come on answer me. Where does most of the money come from?"

Pepper looked at the floor, and spoke in a low voice. "Prostitution, Sir."

"Finally we have reached the moment of truth," said the coroner.

"It is not illegal in New South Wales, Sir."

"I am aware of that Mr. Pepper. But are you aware that it is not legal if the women are coerced?"

"Some seem happy to take part."

"Could it be because they would otherwise not receive food? Mr. McBride has already told us that Lucy, for example, went hungry because she would not take part in certain activities. It would not take an intelligent person long to work out what that was."

Pepper did not answer.

"I am going to advise the police to look into the matter. You may leave the witness box."

The coroner read his notes for a minute or two, and then spoke. "The court will reconvene tomorrow morning at ten o'clock." He rose and left the courtroom.

McBride was pleased about the easy hours of the inquest. Now he had time to visit the gallery before he had dinner this evening.

The gallery was busy. McBride had received some good publicity, including another write up in the *Herald* yesterday. The gallery owner was sitting in a chair against the wall, smiling at the numbers circulating. McBride went over and spoke a few words, mentioning that he had to attend the inquest regarding the Dulong fire. The gallery owner expressed his concern over the affair, and asked how much longer the inquest was expected to last. McBride said that he didn't know, and immediately spotted Sergeant Jack Hopkins walking in through the doorway.

"Here's someone who may know," he said, and called the sergeant over.

"Hello, Mr. McBride, I thought I might see you here."

"We were just wondering how much longer the inquest over the Dulong fire might last? Would you like to take an educated guess?"

"Well, tomorrow I understand there are the autopsy reports on the bodies that were buried on the site. Then there will be a summing up by the coroner. Tomorrow should be the final day. I came here to view your paintings, after reading so much about you."

McBride walked round the exhibits with the sergeant. Apart from the Sydney townscape paintings, there were animal paintings from African safari parks, and some London townscapes. "I see you've sold an awful lot of these," said Hopkins, pointing to the red dots that indicated a sold painting.

"Just as well," said McBride. "About half the selling price goes to the gallery, and half of the remainder goes to my agent. So I only get a quarter."

McBride changed the subject. "Any word on Harold Fox, the man who broke bail?"

"Not yet. Someone's probably hiding him. Australia's a big continent. Maybe we'll never catch him."

"I'm so mad about those young girls that have never had a chance to grow up like most children, it makes my blood boil. I bet I could find him. I would slap a few people he knew to make them tell me, and follow the trail. I used to be in the SAS before I was a painter. Unfortunately you can't break the law, because you uphold it. It's easier for me."

"I could look the other way, but the rest of the force wouldn't, so you would have to take care. Don't kill anyone would be my advice. Leave it to us to punish the guy. Phone me if you find him, and I'll come quickly, wherever you are in Australia. I honestly don't think he would get overseas without a passport, and he hasn't got one."

Hopkins' cell phone was ringing. He pulled it out of his pocket, held it to his ear.

"Yes." He listened in silence for a minute. "Get down to his caravan, see if he's there. Phone me when you get there. Go now."

He put the phone away, his face showing strain. He turned to McBride. "Pepper didn't report to the Dulong station, as he was supposed to do. I told the local man to get up to the sect."

"He got a roasting from the coroner this afternoon. The future doesn't look good for him."

"Exactly. That is what worries me. I should get a call back within the next few minutes."

"Can I tempt you to have a coffee? I'm going to have one," McBride said.

They moved over to the sales desk. There was a steaming coffee jug on a table with cups and saucers on a tray. They sat down on a nearby couch drinking coffee and waiting for Hopkins' phone to ring.

Chapter 20

They chatted to the gallery owner whilst they waited for Hopkins' phone to ring. Just as McBride was in the middle of a sentence he heard the phone's shrill noise.

Hopkins had the phone to his ear before the second ring, listened quietly for several minutes.

Then he said, "I'll have a word with the Social Services here in Sydney. Will you hang around there until I get back to you?" He put the phone back in his pocket.

"It's bad news, McBride. Stan Burrows, the local cop, you remember, went straight up to Pepper's caravan as I asked. It was in darkness, no lights on. He peered through the window, could see Pepper had strung himself up. He smashed the door in, cut him down, managed to get the rope off his neck. He had no heartbeat so Stan carried out CPR to no avail. He had phoned for the emergency response team at the hospital, and carried on with the CPR. Sometimes even after half an hour or more, you can save a life. Obviously he couldn't get back to me while he was doing that. The emergency men came and had a defibrillator. They tried about ten times, but he couldn't get Pepper's heart restarted. Stan is asking what we do about the homeless girls with no leader. I'm going to speak to the Social Services here. Come with me, if you like. The whole business started with you, and I want to talk to you further about finding Fox."

They went back to the police station, and Hopkins said, "I must try and sort out some accommodation for the Dulong girls. I'm thinking a battered wives sort of home, if Social Services can find me something. I'm not worried about the older adults, they can stay on in the caravans. But the girls, as I call them, have lived terrible lives, they are damaged souls, and need protection. You were at the court today, did you hear them giving evidence?"

"I did. It's even worse for me, because I met Lucy, who died and is buried at the Dulong home. I grieve for the life she led. Anything I can help you with in order to rehouse the other girls, tell me."

Hopkins rubbed his chin, thinking but then he said, "I hear what you say, but first let me make this phone call."

He obviously had contacts, inevitably due to his career, and he looked in his notebook before lifting his landline phone and dialing. He first apologized for contacting the person he was talking to, at home but it was an urgent matter. McBride mentally switched off, because he didn't want to eavesdrop. He picked up a police magazine from a side table and idly leafed through it. It was extremely boring to a layman, and after a few minutes dropped it back on the table and wandered to the window and looked out. Although it was dark by now, the street lights were on, and there was plenty of traffic, both pedestrian and motorized. McBride became immersed in his own thoughts, and jumped when Hopkins came up behind him.

"A penny for your thoughts?"

"They are not even worth that. I was waiting for you to finish your call, and obviously you have done that." He turned to face the policeman.

"Well, I'm now waiting for a call back, and I must say that it looks promising.

"That call was to a councilor in charge of the Social Services in Sydney. There are three premises that are called women's refuges. When women are beaten by their husbands, and it happens quite often you may be surprised to learn, the state invites the women to live for a while in a refuge, until they have got alternative accommodation. It seems that at the moment the men aren't beating their women quite as much, and so they have a home that isn't being used. They are prepared to open it up to house our girls for perhaps a month or even more, until we can find suitable accommodation. Bear in mind that we might not find Fox, and even if we do he can hardly run the cult when he'll be in jail for a number of years, or even life. And of course, Pepper is dead."

***

Hopkins and McBride were both standing on the steps of the refuge. They had met the matron earlier in the evening. Stan Burrows, at the cult premises, had called the guarding angels and the girls together, and the police of NSW had decided that the girls be immediately relocated to a refuge in Sydney. A minibus had been hired from a local cab company, and the vehicle would be here shortly. The time when Burrows made his speech was seven in the evening.

McBride looked at his watch. Ten thirty-five. "Should be here shortly," he said to Hopkins. It had been Hopkins' idea to be present when the girls arrived. He had changed into a police uniform at the station, and now looked rather grand. McBride was still in his suit he had worn all day. At least they had eaten, at a pub near the police station, before they arrived at the refuge, and been given a tour of the facilities by the matron. The place had a homely feel, well-furnished, with en suite bedrooms for two people sharing and with luxurious public areas.

The minibus turned into the street and pulled to a stop in front of the steps to the door. Hopkins ran down the stairs, and pulled open the passenger door at the rear of the vehicle. As the girls descended onto the path, Hopkins shook hands with each of them. The driver started unloading their luggage. Each of them had an identical case with a large label bearing their first names. As they walked up the steps, McBride was suddenly aware that none of them had last names.

In the large lobby, the girls were looking nervous, shuffling their feet like nine-year-olds, rather than twenty-nine-year olds. The matron addressed them collectively, welcoming them to Sydney and their new, if temporary, home. She went around giving each of them a numbered key. Then she took them to their rooms, a snaking column of ladies walking down a corridor following the matron leaving the lobby suddenly empty. Except for McBride and Hopkins, who walked together down to the street. They were each going in different directions. They parted with the promise of meeting up at the inquest the following day. And McBride made his way back to his apartment, thinking of Lucy with No Last Name

CHAPTER 21

McBride was up later the next morning than he had planned. The previous day had seemed to go on forever. It was gone ten o'clock when he had left Hopkins, the police sergeant, and gone midnight before he had got to bed. He rushed around getting his breakfast before setting off for what he hoped would be the last day of the inquest.

He got there at just before ten, and sneaked into a seat in the public area. The place was packed, people were expecting the best entertainment, and of course, the verdict. At ten o'clock on the dot, the coroner entered carrying his pile of paperwork which he slammed onto his desk, before carefully sitting down in his chair.

"I am hoping that I will be able to arrive at a verdict today. I am aiming for this morning before a late luncheon, but if it goes on all day, so be it.

"The first witness I call this morning is Mr. George Simmons_who is a pathologist attached to the government laboratories here in Sydney. He was in charge of a group who exhumed the six bodies buried in the apple orchard at land occupied by the Children of Messiah. The cult has been in occupation of the site for forty-one years, so it can be assumed, unless we hear evidence to the contrary, that the bodies were interred by, or with the knowledge of, the Children of Messiah."

Mr. Simmons was not a bespectacled old man, but a six foot tall handsome guy, dressed in sports jacket and flannels, white shirt and a rather gaudy tie. He had curly brown hair and an infectious smile. He came into the witness box, and put a business case on the shelf in front of him, pulled out a cardboard file case, closed the case and put it on the floor. In front of him was the file. He put on a fashionable pair of glasses, and began to read from his papers.

"The six exhumed bodies from the grounds of the Children of Messiah were taken to the Sydney mortuary, where they were examined. They had been buried in a line, the oldest burial being the one nearest to the building which has now been destroyed by fire. This body was of a young child, estimated age at death six years. She had been strangled, and this was the cause of death. The next burial was of a girl aged about ten who had suffered bad internal injuries in the vaginal area, and her death was probably caused by excessive bleeding. The remaining four bodies died of starvation. The full documentation I now hand over to the court." He handed the file to the coroner.

The coroner said, "Where, currently are the bodies?"

"In refrigeration at the laboratories, Sir. Are they to be reburied on the original site, or at any of the cemeteries in the Sydney area?"

"I shall recommend in my report that they be reinterred in a public cemetery, together with headstones paid for out of the public purse."

"I have to announce that Christopher Pepper, the leader of the sect, took his own life last evening by hanging. He was discovered by Constable Burrows of the Dulong constabulary, after he had failed to report to the police station in accordance with his terms of bail."

"My conclusions will be made known to the authorities. I will report that the cause of death of the eleven members of the sect was due to the effects of fire, mainly by smoke inhalation, in some cases by burning. The rescue was hindered because they were in locked bedrooms. This was the fault of the late Mr. Pepper, but he may have been following the previous instructions of Mr. Harold Fox. Regarding the deaths of the interred girls, the young ones who had been buried the longest, were undoubtedly the victims of one or more pedophiles, the likeliest being Harold Fox, who was in charge at the time. Of the other four buried bodies, their death in all likelihood caused by their deprivation of food. Mr. McBride has given evidence that food was not given to certain members of the sect unless they took part in prostitution. He was told this by the last of the victims, a girl called Lucy. The prostitution was therefore illegal because the ladies were under duress. In all probability the prostitution started under the rule of Harold Fox, but I am sure this can be ascertained by the police. I cannot call Mr. Harold Fox, because his whereabouts are not known to the police. I therefore close this inquest."

***

McBride stood up and looked about the room for Sergeant Hopkins. He was down the same row at the end. McBride stood back when he got out from the public seats, and waited for Hopkins.

"Hello, McBride. I thought you hadn't made it this morning."

"I was further along your row. I needed to see you because you said a couple of times yesterday that you had something to tell me, but you never got round to it. But we did have a busy day."

"You are not kidding. Come and have a coffee," he looked at his watch. "No, dammit, it's way past lunchtime. Come and have something to eat."

"Okay," said McBride, "but I'm buying."

They walked out through the rush of people spilling on to the footpath. McBride led the policeman round the next corner and into the Italian café. The woman behind the refrigerated counter greeted him. McBride said to Hopkins, "I'm having a panini: ham and cheese. What about you?"

"That will be fine. Also a black coffee and a glass of water."

McBride told the lady and she wrote the order, stuck it on a hook above her, took two side plates, put some olives and bread on each plate. "That is to be going on with," she said and smiled before she turned round to the espresso machine, and McBride waited for the coffees, while Hopkins went over to a table, grabbing two glasses of water and cutlery on the way. McBride thought: that guy has been here before. He brought the coffees over, and sat down.

"Now tell me what you didn't have time for yesterday."

"I did some research on Harold Fox, to give you something of a start in your search for him. I went through old records. You probably knew he was arrested a few times mostly for sexual offenses. He was born in Dulong, but he spent some time in other places." He popped an olive into his mouth, chewed on it. He dug into his jacket pocket, pulled a small notepad out. "Make some notes if you like."

"I'd better do that. Can you give me his life tours, chronologically?"

"Sure. He went to school in Dulong, got himself expelled for sexually interfering with girls. Knocked around with Willy Green, he owns the gas station in Dulong."

McBride chipped in. "The guy with the broken pumps, guesses the prices?"

"That's him. Then he had to get out of town, or be arrested. So he turns up in Melbourne. Doesn't register for school though, and he's only twelve. Gets a job in the fruit market, wheeling barrows about. He stays in a rooming house, but gets chucked out after a couple of years for having women in his room, not once or twice, but with great regularity. By this time, he could get mistaken for an eighteen-year-old."

He was interrupted by the cook fetching the panini. Each one had a side salad. The café was good value, and the full tables were the result. McBride finished making notes before he attacked his food.

"Carry on," said McBride.

"He came back to Dulong for a while. Got arrested and jailed for rape. So he was out of circulation for three years. Prison outside of Sydney."

McBride interrupted. "Were they just local prisoners?"

"His co-prisoners? Yes they were."

"So no friends in other parts of the country then?"

"Not at that time. So when he got out of jail he's, what, eighteen. Almost immediately, he's off to Perth. We know that's where he went, because he was caught on a couple of pedophile charges. He was jailed there, ten years this time. And he served all of it, which shows he was not a model prisoner. When he was released he was thirty, because he'd been in Perth for twelve years including his prison time. He comes back to Dulong, and he's got the idea for a cult. He told Willy about it, at great length. But Willy had no interest in it. He thinks that Fox was trying to get some investment from him. He was already in business with the gas station. He kicks around for another couple of years, making the odd trip out of town. He must have obtained some cash because he came back after a few months. Might have stolen some cash, but we never heard if he did. Anyway he comes back and buys the fifty acre plot up the road from Dulong. I looked up the land registry, and he paid cash.

"So, he pays a hundred dollars, and gets a mortgage for the rest. After about a year, he's get some more money together and he employs one or two guys to build the wooden cabin. He helps down there every day."

Hopkins paused to eat his panini and to drink the coffee. McBride carried on making notes, and caught up before Hopkins started talking again.

"He slipped off the radar. Turns out now that he was still up to his old tricks but the victims were imprisoned so to speak, so they didn't get to speak out. Trouble is, Australia's too damned big to police. With the population spread out so thinly, you'd have to end up with one policeman for every three people."

McBride spoke. "It's given me some leads. Every lead stretches to another one, until you've got a spider's web, and the spider is there in the middle. That's what we used to reckon in the SAS Regiment."

"Interesting," said Hopkins. "But I wouldn't like the job. Anyway I wish you luck. If you get stuck phone me and I'll try and help." He stood up. "I'll have to go, there's always more policing then there is time. Good luck."

McBride went back to the counter, spoke to the girl. "Excuse me, but do you know where I would find the Sydney prison?"

"I sure wouldn't. My God, I've never been to prison, and no-one I know has."

"I apologize."

"Ask your policeman friend who has just left."

"I will," said McBride and he gave her a wave as he left. That was a damn stupid question to ask. And as he walked to his apartment, he began to do some mental arithmetic. Fox was seventy-three and went to jail aged eighteen. That was fifty-five years ago. There would be no serving officers who were at the jail when Fox was there. He could scrub that one. Fox's time in Melbourne could be discounted. That too was just too long ago.

He should start with Willy at the Dulong gas station, which should lead to Fox's manservant, for starters. Then he could go to the burned out ruins of the sect, and speak to a few guarding angels. He'd better do that quickly, because he reckoned they would disperse. They wouldn't be getting paid in future he bet.

CHAPTER 22

McBride left the café, walked back to the apartment packed a small case, walked down the road and once more hired a Toyota Auris from Hertz.

He drove through the mountains to Dulong, arriving at six thirty in the evening as dusk was falling. The lights over the petrol pumps in the gas station were on, two pools of light on the concrete. He pulled in and within seconds Willy stepped out of the shed.

McBride got out of the car, stretching after driving four hours from Sydney. Willy suddenly recognized him and he grinned, showing yellowing teeth.

"Fill it up?"

"Yes please." He dug a ten dollar note out and gave it to Willy. Willy grinned again.

"You know the pump's still broken, eh?"

"I didn't think you got it fixed. There could be more cash if you answered me a few questions."

Willy looked serious. "Maybe I won't answer them. Depends on what you ask." The pump clicked off. "That was just ten dollars, Sir." And he grinned again. "You want to come to the office, to ask the questions?"

McBride followed the man back to the corrugated steel shed. There was a single bulb above the wooden counter. Willy went behind where his desk was positioned, and McBride followed him, sat in the chair opposite him, the desk between them. The desk top was strewn with paperwork, some of it heaped into untidy piles, the rest covering every inch of the desktop. Since the only light came from the single bulb feet away, McBride's shadow was cast over the desk, whereas Willy had his eyes screwed up, even though the lamp was weak, maybe only 40 watts.

"The big question Willy: where is Harold Fox? You must know he broke his bail, ran away."

"Yes, I did know. But I don't know where he has gone."

"But you might hazard a guess?" McBride pulled a twenty out of his pocket, laid it on the desk on top of a pile of bills.

"I could offer a lot of guesses. I know he's not at home. He could be on his boat f'rinstance."

"Oh, you know he has a boat? The one he keeps in Melbourne?"

"That's the one. You could go look."

"Here's another question. You said Fox came back to Dulong after a long time. Where had he been?"

"When he built the cult, you mean?"

"Yes, that's what I mean. I know he'd been in prison in Sydney. But not that. When he came back to Dulong forty years ago. Where from?"

"Perth."

"Did he ever mention any friends he had there?"

Willy didn't answer for a long time, and McBride was going to ask him again. But then he said, "I think there was a guy who lent him a flat in his house. His name was Billy, I forget the last name, if he ever told me."

"Where is Fox's servant, the guy who answers the door?"

"I don't know. Maybe he's still at the house."

"I thought for some reason he wasn't, that the house is all locked up."

"Don't know," was Willy's reply. McBride could feel that he knew more than he was telling.

"I could beat the hell out you. You might tell me more then."

"Ain't nothing more I can tell you," Willy replied sullenly. McBride stood up suddenly, reached across the desk grabbed Willy by the throat. He began to cough and moan. McBride said, "This is nothing to what I could do." Then he got hold of his shoulders and pulled the man up over the desk, scattering most of the papers onto the floor. He fell on to his knees on McBride's side of the desk, looked up at McBride who hadn't broken a sweat. He said, "You've fucked up my filing." McBride looked down at him.

"You don't know what the word means." Then he heard a loud bell ring. He glanced up at the wall, and a box with a bell on it was vibrating loudly.

"Customer," said Willy, struggling to get off the floor. When he was standing he reached over to a button on the wall, pressed it, and the noise stopped. Willy went out of the door. McBride heard him speak to somebody outside. He strolled to the door and stood outside. Willy was lifting the diesel pump nozzle sticking it into the tank of a seven ton truck. A fat guy was standing by watching him. McBride idly wondered if that pump was broken too. He walked back into the office, the single bulb the only illumination. Away to the back of the building he could see a hydraulic lift with a car on it. The lift was raised so that the wheels of the saloon were at eye level. Away to the left as he stood by the counter was a stores area with dexion racking containing boxes and cans of engine oil and screen-wash. Everything he could see was covered in a film of dust. He looked down at his hands; they were black.

The truck engine started and it drove off. Willy came back through the door, stuffing dollar notes into the front of his overall. He was chewing tobacco again. McBride hoped there was a spittoon near his desk.

"Just two questions I want to ask and then I'll go. But I might be back." McBride stared hard at Willy as they both stood under the light bulb.

"Ask me then," said Willy.

"What is the manservant's name?"

"Danny. Danny Wilton."

"Where does he live?"

"You know where he lives. At Harold Fox's house."

"But when the house is shut up?"

"He might be with his dad, Albert. He's a real old man, lives by himself, in a shack on the road out of Dulong, the road to the cult. The second shack past the speed limit sign."

"Has Albert got a telephone number?"

"Don't be stupid. Of course not. I'm closing up now. You'll have to go."

McBride walked to the door, turned with his hand on the latch . "If you haven't told the truth, I'll be back." And he slammed the door after him.

McBride got into the hire car. He decided to talk to some of the Guarding Agents who should be still living in their temporary caravans at the cult site, tending the farm. Or at least he hoped so.

As he passed the speed limit signs he slowed up, and looked left and right for houses or huts. He passed the first on the left, and then the second. Lights were showing. It was a corrugated roofed wooden hut in rather a dilapidated state. He pulled the car on to the grass verge, got out and walked back to the hut, a distance of maybe a hundred yards.

He knocked on the sun-faded painted door. After a minute or so, the door opened and a stooped old man, leaning heavily on a walking stick, stood there holding the door for extra support. He looked at McBride through rheumy eyes.

"What yer want?"

"Is your son staying with you?"

"Which one?"

"Er, Danny I was looking for."

"I ain't seen him for a long time. He works for Fox, lives in his house. You best call there. Big house, the back of Main Street."

"Fox has gone away. The police want to talk to him, but he doesn't want to talk to them."

"Ain't surprised. I allus told Danny that Fox was a bad one. Always will be."

"When did you last see Danny?"

"When his mother died, that's ten year ago."

"Okay, sorry to have bothered you," McBride said and went back up the road to the car.

He knew then that going to the cult property would be a waste of time. Two of the people there were the guardians of Lucy, and he couldn't meet them again without beating them up, probably killing them for what they had allowed to happen to Lucy. And the rest of the angels would be useless wasters who had just been along with the cult for the free ride.

He decided to go to the Fox house in Dulong. Maybe the manservant really was there although it might well appear to be empty. The only danger would be burglar alarms linked direct to the police. He smiled to himself as he drove, at the thought of Stan Burrows trying to find him. Only in his early fifties but so unfit.

The Fox house stood large and imposing, one or two streetlights down the street, but not outside the big house. As he got near, on foot, after leaving his car in the market square, he saw that there were closed shutters over all the windows at the front of the house. On each side of the house were tall walls enclosing the gardens behind. In the middle of the wall to the left of the house, was a wooden door with the word *tradesmen* painted on the white surface in black paint. McBride looked up and down the street. Empty. No CCTV cameras that he could see, so he approached the white door, and tried the door catch. The door opened smoothly on its hinges, and he quickly went in and closed the door. This was a bit too easy.

McBride looked up at the house now to the right of him. One of the windows on the ground floor had a light showing behind drawn curtains. He tried the door at the end of the path to the house. It was locked. He pulled out a lock pick from his pocket, not an instrument to be discovered by a policeman, but then the pocket he kept it in was fairly well hidden. He poked in the lock, and was pleased to find it a three lever lock, not too hard to pick with a little time. He felt the levers give at last to his probing, and the handle turned. He pushed gently at the door, opening it very slowly. He went quickly in, pulling the door closed behind him.

He was in a short corridor with an un-shaded overhead bulb. To the left, a wall. To the right a short passage and a solid door. Ahead, a room without any lighting, although a switch on the wall. He could see at least one stainless rack loaded with cartons. And to one side a large stainless steel refrigerator, or maybe a freezer. No sound except for the slight hum of a compressor in the machine. He took a step forward, put his hand on the shelf edge of the rack and inched his way forward into darkness. He took his time because he didn't want to bump into anything which would make a noise. His eyes became accustomed to the low light, and he came to a door ahead in the far wall. He turned the handle, and pushed. He entered the kitchen. He wished that he had brought a torch. He felt to one side of the door, then the other. His hand felt a light switch. He held his breath, ready to attack, and flicked the switch, momentarily blinded. Multiple ceiling spotlights shone out. Stainless steel tabling, a six burner range, combi-oven, sinks, all the equipment of an upmarket kitchen met his eyes. All dazzlingly clean in the white lights, the stainless steel reflecting the lights in the ceiling. He heard footsteps, careful tread, cautious but soon to meet the doorway behind him. McBride stood still looking down the kitchen the way he had come. And into the doorway came a man he had never seen before. But he looked like his father. A much younger version of his father he now never visited. Danny, the son of Albert Wilton who McBride had visited earlier that evening.

Chapter 23

"Mr. Wilton? Nice to meet you." McBride pushed the edge of his bottom onto the stainless steel table beside him, to show that he wasn't scared.

"Who gave you permission to be in here? You a burglar, as well as a painter?"

"Clever. You recognize me, eh?"

"How did you know my name?"

"You look a lot like your dad who I met earlier tonight. He didn't send his love though. Said you hadn't called round for ten years." McBride shook his head ruefully.

Danny Wilton glowered at McBride. "How did you get in here?"

"Well, I admit I was trying to find out if Harold Fox, or anyone else was in the house. At the front it is all closed up, as you know. I saw the tradesmen's entrance, tried the gate and it was open. You should have locked it, you know. You could get a whole stream of people come calling who don't like Fox."

"But I locked the house door at the side."

"Yes. There is that. I had to jiggle the lock, but I didn't break anything. I was only walking around trying to find somebody. Will you talk to me about Fox? Unless he's still here, in which case I would like to talk with him."

"Of course he isn't here. The police are after him because he's broken his bail. As you know. And of course, when he didn't report to the station, Stan Burrow was straight round here like a greyhound out of the trap."

"Tell me where he's likely gone. Or didn't he tell you? I bet he didn't."

"No, of course not."

"But you might have a good idea. How long have you worked for him? Ten years, twenty years?"

"Twenty years, near enough. I honestly don't know where he's gone. But he had a contact in Perth, so who knows?"

"Do you have a name in Perth?"

"On the phone he calls him Billy. Come through to my room. I can't let you walk through the house."

McBride slipped off the table walked after Wilton, who was going back the way he'd come. As McBride had surmised, he lived through the door on the right from the side door. To get to his accommodation he was only about three steps inside the house. A true servant, Wilton stood aside to let McBride into the room first. It was a large living room, pleasantly furnished, big TV set in the corner of the room, not switched on. There was a novel open and face down on a table next to a sofa.

He waved McBride to the sofa, and seated himself on an upholstered chair in a corner.

"Mr. Fox left a telephone number up there on the mantelpiece, case I needed him." He pointed and McBride looked over to the shelf, and behind a pottery figurine was a piece of paper. Just at that very moment, a bell sounded elsewhere in the building.

"Damn, wait there. That's the outside door." Wilton was out of his chair, through the door, closing it behind him.

McBride had heard the bell ring, and thought it coincided too neatly with his attention being diverted just at that moment to the fireplace. In any case, if someone came to the door, why would he answer it? The house was supposed to be empty.

It didn't hurt to be safe rather than sorry, so he immediately walked across the room and stood just to the right of the hinge side of the door Wilton had gone through. He pressed himself to the wall and waited. Moments later somebody was pushing open the door and then Wilton with his back to McBride was in the room with a shot gun on his hip, and a puzzled look on his face as he turned it one way and the other, looking for McBride.

McBride chopped at Wilton's neck with the edge of his hand, and Wilton collapsed on the carpet. McBride caught the gun as it fell from his hand, went to the window, opened it and flung the shotgun into the garden. After shutting the window, he went back to Wilton's body which was still on the floor, bent down and felt for a pulse in the neck. It was there, very slow, and Wilton was still unconscious. McBride went to the mantelpiece. The piece of paper was only a shopping list.

McBride left Wilton still on the floor, and walked out of the room, turning on lights as he went. He found the main staircase, climbed to the first floor, decided to turn right, it was purely random. If he didn't find Fox's bedroom that way, he would retrace his steps and go the other way. He came to a doorway. The end of the corridor. The door was locked, which McBride thought was promising. He got out his pick lock again. An easier lock this time, he barely missed a beat before he was through the door, switching on the light as he went. The large king bed was unmade, just as Fox had got up and left for wherever. McBride swiveled round and saw a bureau against the wall opposite the window. It was standing open, the desk lid down on the

stops that come out when the top comes down. The desk was a jumble of items, bills, letters opened and unopened. He pulled open the top drawer, and stared in disbelief. The drawer was stuffed to the top with banknotes, most of it high denomination as far as he could see. He closed it again. The next drawer was full of pornography. He didn't want to look any further. None of this was helping to find Fox. He really needed phone records of the calls he had made. And McBride had no way of finding that. But he knew a man who could.

He switched out the bedroom light, and made his way downstairs, switching off lights as he went.

When he got to Wilton's room, the door was still open, but Wilton was on the sofa looking dazed. McBride walked over to him stood looking at him. Wilton looked up, puzzled.

"I must have collapsed. Did I?" Now stroking the side of his neck. "And what about…what about—"

McBride leaned down over the sofa and helped him to his feet. He escorted him to his chair in the corner, noticing the bell push on the wall next to the chair.

"If you are all right, I'll leave now," said McBride, and walked out of the room turned left and left the house the way he had entered.

He walked back to the market square, got into the hire car. It was still only

eight o'clock, and he decided to return to Sydney. Then tomorrow he could visit John Hopkins at the police station there.

McBride didn't wake next morning until just gone nine. A heavy day previously including eight hours' driving had wearied him. Once out of bed he phoned Sergeant Hopkins even before he dressed. Hopkins sounded pleased to hear from him and said he would be in the station all morning if McBride wanted to drop by. The first thing McBride did when dressed was to return the rental car. The second thing was buy some breakfast at a nearby café. Finally, at just gone eleven, he walked into the police station. He hardly had time to read the crime posters, before John Hopkins was in front of him smiling.

"Good to see you, McBride, you want to tell me where Fox is?"

"I wish. But we are a bit further down the road." He stood up.

Hopkins said, "Come along to my office."

When they were both comfortably seated, and Hopkins had put two coffees on the table, McBride began.

"I went back to Dulong yesterday, asking questions. Most people thought Fox's house was all shut up. But it's not. True, from the front all the shutters are over the windows. But I got round the back in the garden, and there was a light shining. The manservant, Wilton, is still living there."

"That guy Burrows is a lousy cop."

"Maybe the job's a bit much for him. He does seem to accept things at face value. Anyway, according to Willy at the gas station, and the manservant, Fox has a connection with a guy in Perth called Billy. No last name forthcoming, though."

Hopkins smirked. "There's a lot of people in Perth. 'bout two million, guess half of them are fellows. Not all called Billy, mind." He laughed.

"This is why I'm here to see you. Are you able to get lists of calls from the phone people, of calls in and out of a private line, say for a date just before and just after you bailed old Fox?"

"Not easy, got to have a good reason for asking. And, since I'm ahead of you already, you'd want the addresses that go with the numbers."

"You can feed the numbers into the internet and get the answers."

"Could do a few years ago. Now it's not so easy. If a person doesn't want his number coming up with an address, he can have it removed. You can imagine who those people would be, the ones with something to hide."

"True. But this is why it's me doing the leg work. You get the numbers, I'll get the addresses, but don't ask how."

Hopkins opened his computer with his card in the slot. "You wouldn't know the dates?"

"Jesus, you locked him up and then bailed him. Look it up."

"Just trying to make it easier. Ah, I have it. So a week before and a week after?"

He left the screen open to refer to, and phoned a friend at the Sydney exchange. He gave the address in Dulong, and the name Harold Fox.

When he put the phone down he said to McBride, "He's emailing the answer in an attachment. Might be half an hour he says." He looked at his wristwatch. "You could buy me lunch while we wait."

They walked over to the Italian café that they had used when they attended the inquest. It was as busy as before, but they found themselves a small table tucked away in the back.

While they were waiting for the food, McBride said, "I found out that Wilton had a double barreled shotgun in the house. You might want to get someone see if he's got a license."

"He threatened you with it?"

"He went out of the room to get it. I knew he was up to something, so I got behind the door."

"And?" said Hopkins, demolishing a bread roll, popping olives.

"I chucked the gun out of the window."

"Marvellous."

The old chef came bustling through the tables, plates held high, calling, "Two tagliatelle."

McBride stuck his arm in the air.

While they ate, they fell silent.

Back in Hopkins' office at the police station, he pushed his card in the keyboard, and the screen powered up. There were three emails in the queue. Hopkins brought them up. He clicked on the one from the phone company, clicked again and there was a list about a page long, with telephone numbers in a column. Hopkins reached out, switched the printer on, and a single sheet of paper fell into the tray. He picked it up, passed it to McBride.

McBride felt in his pocket, pulled out a pencil, smoothed the paper on the desk. "What's the Perth numbers?"

"Prefixed 853 through to 869, from memory." McBride was silent, going through the list, ticking certain lines. "That's about twenty calls from and to Perth, most of them the same number."

"If there's only one number you want an address for I could get it for you," said Hopkins, feeling generous after his lunch. McBride took the number that appeared several times in both directions, and copied the number at the bottom of the paper, handed it to the policeman. Hopkins looked at the paper, made a phone call,

consulted the list and read out the eight digit number. He scrawled on the bottom of the list: William B. Henry, 176 Blue Grass Highway, Perth."

McBride stood up, gave a cheery wave, and left Hopkins' office, clutching the paper. When he got to the foyer, he carefully folded the paper, and popped it into his wallet.

Back in his apartment he fired up his laptop, and checked flights Sydney to Perth. Flight time is two hours, and he found a flight leaving at 7pm. He checked in by phone and booked a seat. He packed another case and took a cab to the airport. Finding Fox was proving a non-stop search round the continent.

CHAPTER 24

The Perth plane was only about half full. McBride had an aisle seat. Next to him there was an empty seat, and a youngish woman by the window. The plane took off on time at 7.05 pm when it was nearly dark, a red sky near the horizon in the direction it headed. As it reached cruising height, the sun reappeared, long sunbeams reaching into the plane interior.

As soon as the belt signs were extinguished, the girl down the row had her finger on the bell above her. The stewardess came down the aisle, leaned over above McBride and pressed the call lamp.

"May I have a double whisky please," she said. When she got the drink, she slurped half of it in one gulp, before putting the glass on the tray in front of her.

McBride thought that either she was a nervous flyer, or an alcoholic. He opened a book he'd brought with him and settled back.

Ten minutes later the girl was ringing the bell for a refill. She felt she needed to explain to McBride, he thought, because she spoke.

"I'm sorry to be swigging alcohol like this, but I hate flying. I hate it so much that I only do two flights a year, and they're for business reasons. I've a ground-based job with Qantas." McBride smiled. "I knew you would smile. I can't leave, the job is too good. I tell myself I can do it. But it doesn't help. When we are coming in to land I use the sick bag. I tell you just so you can look the other way."

"Have you been to see your GP, get him to prescribe some tablets? You're not the only person who needs a sedative."

"For me the sedative is alcohol. It's the only time I drink. Honestly."

He considered what she had said while she sipped her second drink. The plane had been in the air no more than twenty minutes. If she carried on like this she'd be as drunk as a skunk well before the plane landed.

As they had started their descent to Perth, the captain announced that due to crosswinds it may be a bumpy landing. However, the captain didn't sound as though he were worried about this. McBride's neighbor was, and immediately reached for the sick bag, and McBride heard several loud noises. The plane landed with only a slight bump, and taxied quickly to the terminal building. The girl used the time to wipe her face with a large handkerchief, and as McBride stood waiting in the aisle for her to precede him, she was carrying the sick bag, and handing it to the steward. She then vanished into the plane's toilet, presumably to re-apply make-up. McBride hurried through the airport, not wanting to have to share a cab to the hotel.

There were only two or three people waiting for taxis, and McBride climbed into the third one to draw up at the rank. Unusually it was driven by a young man with an Australian accent. When McBride asked for his downtown hotel, the driver said, "From England, I guess. This your first time in the country?"

"Yes, first visit but I've been in Sydney and Melbourne for a few weeks. I'm beginning to feel I belong."

"Yes, it's a great place to be, and Perth is one of the best. You got business in the city?"

"Not this time. I'm searching for someone who's skipped bail."

"You're a cop?"

McBride laughed. "Not exactly. I just don't want this guy to get away from something really bad he's done. I'm acting in a citizen role, really."

The driver swung the cab into the pull-in to the hotel.

McBride said, "If you just hang on here, I'll book in and come right out again. There's an address in the suburbs I need to go."

"Sure. No trouble." The Australian keenness to help.

McBride sped out of the hotel automatic doors minus his luggage, opened the cab door, grinned at the driver. "Ready to go," he said, and handed the driver a slip of paper with the address he'd written down in the police station.

"This is a bad area." The driver tilted the paper towards the window to read it.

"A real bad area. Late Victorian large houses, converted to bedsits."

McBride looked the driver in the eye. "I'm fit, not afraid of a fight."

"These guys don't always fight fair."

"Neither do I, when necessary."

"I'm only warning you, mate. Be a shame for you to be badly beaten up. Drugs is a lot of the problem."

McBride used an Australian reply: "No worries."

The skyscraper district was soon behind them, and the road became potholed, street lighting further apart. But trees grew on the sidewalks. There were people about. First they traversed a red light district, women on the road edge, bobbing to smile into the back of the cab. Then the district improved slightly with one or two bars and shops, and large detached houses converted for multiple occupation where the driver pulled to the side of the road .The driver pointed to the meter, and McBride handed over dollars, included a tip.

"Here goes," he said as he opened the door, and waved to the cabbie as he pulled away into the traffic.

He could see that he had been dropped right outside the address on the paper. The house interior lights showed in about half of the three floors of windows.

Next door to the house was a terrace of shops, the end one converted into a bar, with neon beer signs in the windows. McBride made for the bar. It was as good a place as any to start the search.

The door squeaked loudly as he opened it, but no-one looked round. The place was about half full, most of the people at the bar counter, mostly standing leaning with their arms on the top, clutching pints of beer. A barman was wiping the bar top, but only sloshing the liquid about, there was that much around. The sound level was high, most people shouting at their neighbors to be heard.

McBride shoved himself between two men to get to the counter, and waved a dollar note. Some minutes later he caught the eye of a middle aged chunky woman who came along the back of the bar. She pulled the sweat-wet hair back out of her face.

"Can I get you something, honey?"

McBride gave her a smile: "Pint, please."

"Pale ale?"

"Sure." She took a glass from the shelf, filled it from a hose. The beer spilled out onto the counter. She wiped some of the dregs away with a cloth, then took the note, and turned to the till, put the change on the bar, smiled and rushed off to the next sale.

Next to McBride, a youngish guy was drinking his beer, taking long sips, eyes looking nowhere in particular.

"Hey, Buster, I wonder whether you can help me." He gave him a gentle nudge so that the guy would know where the question was coming from. "I'm a stranger round here. I'm looking for a guy called William B Henry. Do you know him?"

"He's an old guy comes in here most days, he's older than you." *Thanks thought McBride, I'm only forty one for God's sake.* He looked again at the man next to him. He was only about twenty. Oh, well…

"So is he in tonight?"

"Nah, too busy for him at this time. Comes in most days across lunchtime. That's when you would catch him"

"Great. So he lives next door doesn't he?"

"Yeah. Right."

"So I could call on him, right."

"Suppose so. I never thought." Well you wouldn't, you're just too young.

"What flat number is it?'

"Just on the ground floor. All of the ground floor. Doesn't have a number. Just says MANAGER on the door."

The house next door had a list of bedsits on the side of the door, with bell pushes alongside each number. The door was locked. McBride had rattled it. He pressed a number at random. Almost immediately, a voice spoke through the speaker: "Yeah."

"Can you let me in, mate? Forgotten me keys." He heard the latch go, and pushed open the door. He stepped inside. Away to the left there was a staircase, linoleum treads, aluminum protectors on the stair edges. Ahead was another heavy door with a plate on it. MANAGER. He rapped on the door. After a few moments, just when he was going to knock again he heard a padding noise, like someone in slippers, or even stocking feet walking on the carpet. The door lock clicked and the man on the other side threw open the door. He wasn't afraid of anyone who came calling.

McBride looked at him. Big guy, fiftyish, going to seed slightly, bit of a paunch but some useful muscles in his arms. He stood there waiting for McBride to speak. This could last for a while, some sort of competition. McBride gave in without rancor.

"Hello Mr. Henry is it? Hope I've found the right person. We have a mutual friend."

Mr. Henry seemed to have lost his voice, or he was still playing the game. McBride conceded defeat and started talking.

"I've come calling because we've a mutual friend, name of Harold Fox. Can I come in?" Complete capitulation, he'd acknowledged it.

Henry pushed the door a little wider, turned and led the way. He had his own private lobby to himself, bigger than the public lobby, five doors off. He took the first on the left, left the door open for McBride to follow. A nice airy room, two outside windows, plush furniture. He might own a tacky rooming house, but you wouldn't know it inside his living quarters.

Henry pointed to a chair, and sat down on the other chair opposite. He was a lot calmer than McBride would have been if the positions were reversed. Surely the man was not on drugs. But in this area of town who was to know?

"I came over from Sydney where I've been working. I know you've been on the phone a lot with Harold recently. I also know that you knew him a long time ago."

Henry spoke. "Harold was my father's friend. He helped him a lot, especially near the end of my father's life. That's something I would rather not talk to you about. But when Harold Fox phoned me completely out of the blue a few weeks ago, I remembered who he was."

"Why did he get in touch with you?"

"You are obviously searching for the guy yourself, so you can probably guess why he phoned."

McBride made up his mind. "Yes, I'll come clean. I know that he's skipped police bail. I've made it my job to catch him. I must say the police won't. You going to beat me?"

"He still did something for my father that he need not have done. Completely beyond the call of duty. Anyway he isn't in Perth now. That much I will tell you."

"Tell me what town or city he's gone to, and I'll get out of your hair now. I'll be gone immediately. If you don't tell me, I'm going to beat you up. Honest to God. Don't think I can't do it."

"I've fought a fair few people in my time," said Billy Henry.

McBride stood up. "Come on, tell me where Fox has gone, or fight."

McBride didn't think he would, but he also didn't think he would tell. He hated this sort of situation. The guy was behaving rationally, and it would be against the grain for McBride to hit him.

McBride had stood up, and was towering over Billy. Suddenly Billy was on his feet, startling McBride. But only for a second and then McBride had lashed out with his fist, aiming at Billy's eye. The punch landed, and Billy stumbled, regained his balance and was coming back, in a boxer's stance, and raining blows at McBride, blows that he avoided fists up and parrying blows, prancing round the room. This went on for some minutes, with blows hitting from both men. McBride guessed eventually that Billy Henry was tiring, his blows landing late, more easily parried.

McBride took pity on the guy, held both his hands up. "Enough! We're just wasting our time beating each other up." They looked at each other. Billy's face had a smashed up look, blood running off his chin, coming from his nose. McBride knew that he was in much the same condition, and that he would get out of bed in the morning with a lot of niggling pains racking his body.

Billy stared at him, then collapsed back into his chair.

"If you say so. You started it."

McBride sat down himself, in the chair he had previously occupied. "Yes, I did start it, and I'm not proud of it.

"Just sit still and hear me out. Forget, for a moment your preconceptions about Harold Fox. I've done a lot of research, even spoken to one of his school mates.

"He was a sex maniac, always assaulting the girls when he was at school. When he left school he prowled round the town raping young women. He was jailed locally, but when he was released he re-offended. The next time he was caught, he was sentenced to three years jail in Sydney.

"When he got out, he came here to Perth. I don't know what he did while he was here, except he spent a lot of time in jail, a police friend of mine told me that. About thirty years ago he returned to Dulong, and must have got some money together because he bought fifty acres of farming land about three miles out of the town. Then he set to building a long wooden building and put up a sign: Children of Messiah. It was a cult. He collected together orphans. Girls, because he liked young girls. Nowadays we call these men pedophiles."

Billy sat still on his chair. He hadn't moved a muscle during the telling of the story. The look on his face told it all. He was repulsed.

"But there's more, Billy. Fox didn't stop at assaulting these young girls. During the fire, and I was there, we had to knock down the girls' bedroom doors, because they were locked in. We saved as many as we could, but thirteen of the girls perished. It gets even worse. When the fire was out, in the dawn of the next day, the firemen found the graves. Six graves. The authorities exhumed the bodies."

McBride paused, and took a handkerchief from his pocket, wiped his eyes.

"I'm sorry, it affects me still. Two of the graves contained the bodies of young girls, aged five or six, and they had died as a result of sexual assault. It seems unbelievable, but it is true. You could look up the coroner's report. The other graves contained the bodies of girls in their twenties. They had died of starvation. They were denied food if they wouldn't engage in prostitution. Yes, Billy, the sect was run as a brothel to pay the enormous rent to keep Fox in his big house with his servants."

For a minute or two there was silence in the room. Eventually Billy said, "I didn't know Fox myself, and I know that my father never knew any of that. If he had, he would never have accepted the blood transfusions."

"Blood transfusions?" said McBride.

"My father's blood group was very rare. The hospital needed to locate someone with the same type. So that they could perform cancer surgery on my father. The hospital found Harold Fox. He willingly provided large transfusions. It was all in vain, though. My father died anyway."

"I'm sorry."

"Don't be. It was a blessing in disguise. I'm glad you told me the story, and in return I'll tell you where Fox has gone."

CHAPTER 25

"Tell me where Harold Fox has gone."

Billy stirred in his chair. Then he said, "He went to Darwin. He had to get out of Perth. The whole city got to know that Harold Fox was a wanted man, that he was here and they had it in for him. Don't ask me how. Someone had spread the word. Fox was living in one of my bedsits. He didn't pay any rent. Seemed to think he was owed. He came down here one night, sat in that very chair.

"He said that he'd been out that morning and that two people had seen him. Knew him from years ago. He thought there was a price on his head. Told me he'd considered going bush. You know what that means? It means setting off into the bush and living rough. Very dangerous if you don't know a lot about the outback. You could be dead within a few days. There's the snakes, the spiders, oh, all manner of things like wild dogs, dingoes, they are called. Run in packs."

"You told him where he could go. Where he would be safe? Safe from discovery?"

"Darwin was somewhere he'd never been before. I advised him to grow some face bristle. That would disguise him. I knew a man who used to live here in Perth. He went up to Darwin, when it was just a small place twenty years ago. The guy did well, put his money into property. Rental accommodation. Residential, for lower middle classes, if you know what I mean."

McBride nodded. He did know what Billy meant. They had a lot of those sort of landlords in Britain. A lot of them had put their pension money into property.

"Well, I gave him the address of my friend, Egbert Bakkar. It's a Dutch name, you know. He's descended from the original Dutch settlers who came to that part of Australia, before Cook discovered the continent. Only the Aborigines preceded them."

"It's up towards the tropics, I should imagine," said McBride.

"Indeed it is. Dry season and a wet season. Should be just coming to the end of the wet season, now."

"Well," said McBride, standing and stretching his tired muscles, "if you'll let me use your bathroom, I'll just clean myself up."

"Sure, it's the room next door to this one. There's a fresh visitor towel hanging on the back of the door. Have a shower, that will make you feel better."

When McBride had finished in the bathroom he returned to the living room feeling almost normal. Billy stood up and handed a piece of paper. "That's Fox's address in Darwin. Please don't tell him that I gave him away."

***

When McBride got outside the rooming house, the noise from the bar was significantly reduced. He glanced at his watch. Ten o'clock. He decided to walk back to the hotel. It was a warm night. He remembered the way the taxi had taken, and he strolled down the road. When he came to the red light district, he took a detour to avoid the pestering he would undoubtedly get from the girls on the street.

It had only taken about twenty minutes to complete the distance to the hotel, and it was a pleasure to stroll through the balmy night air.

At the reception desk, the night clerk had details of flights from Perth to Darwin. Most flights started out at eight fifteen or thereabouts and got into Darwin in time for a late lunch. The price was about 600 GBP return. McBride winced. Mind you his chase sounded as if it was all but over. In a couple of days he should be in Melbourne painting the views for his next exhibition. As he took the elevator for his room he reflected that he had seen virtually nothing of Perth. He had particularly fancied a visit to Kingston Park. Still, he should be back again in the autumn when his Perth exhibition came up.

McBride was up and at the airport at six the next morning. The departure gate was clogged with passengers deciding whether to take the flight or not. Officials were explaining that a cyclone was currently heading towards Darwin, but may alter course before it got anywhere near the city. Cyclones were unpredictable – this one could easily do a U-turn, in which case no worries. The city was battened down, including the airport, just in case. The flight would take off on time, but they may or may not land in Darwin. They could be diverted to Broome.

This uncertainty was scaring some passengers who were cashing in their tickets for refunds. There was no problem with the airline about that. Others, like McBride, decided to take a chance. As a result the plane was less than a third full. McBride had a whole row of seats to himself and decided to take the window seat. He'd never seen a cyclone from the air before, and, come to that, from the ground in real life, just on the television.

The flight was three hours' duration and was uneventful for two and a half hours. The pilot was on the speaker fairly often with updates. They passed Broome, and things were looking hopeful that they would land at Darwin. The sky was filled with high cloud as they approached the city, but over to the east, it was darkening

with the sun casting a golden glow high in the sky, reflecting on angry clouds. The plane as it descended was buffeted by wind. The pilot announced that they were going to try for a landing. The plane came down lurching in the wind, swaying from side to side. The port wheel briefly touched the tarmac and at that moment a gust of wind tossed the plane into the air. The jet engines screamed as the plane fought to regain height, and came round to try again. This time they were down on both wheels, and racing for cover behind the airport passenger terminal. There was a scattering of applause from the passengers.

Once out of the direct wind from the west, in the lee of the terminal, they attached to the ramp and as the passengers warily climbed up the metal slats they felt the tremor caused by the air turbulence, and moved faster to get into the building. The army was in attendance, several soldiers standing by, waiting to haul the passengers into the building. Stern young men, clean shaven, tanned, berets worn at jaunty angles, dressed in jungle patterned denims, gaiters and black dubbin coated boots. The wind moaned over the building.

A uniformed official told passengers they could take refuge in the passenger luggage reclaim area, which was below ground and therefore perfectly safe. Beds had been set up, and food would be served throughout the day. Alternatively, and at their own risk, passengers could transfer to downtown hotels, and army armored buses were available to transport them. McBride decided to go downtown, and tramped through the airport with accompanying troops, part of the way in wood lined passages to protect from flying glass fragments. The terminal had been designed in contemporary fashion with a large glass content without regard to frequent cyclones.

The bus was a dark green colour, matt paint. The windows, including the front window, were covered with metal mesh. The passengers sat on thin hammock like seats provided with safety belts. They set off, and almost immediately the bus was assaulted with flying debris, wooden plywood sheets mainly, but also metal debris and tree branches. The bus drove slowly, the driver steering gingerly round the bigger items of debris on the road. They came upon a building that had collapsed at an intersection; bricks strewn across the road. The bus bumped over them with its huge, reinforced tyres. The journey, painfully slow, took well over an hour, and then the bus was pulling up at the first of the hotels. The hotel windows were protected with thick plywood. McBride thought that this hotel would be as good as any, and joined other passengers disembarking. The rain and wind tore at their clothes as they made the short route into the lobby, where the porter was holding the door open with great difficulty against the buffeting wind.

There was a very short wait at the reception desk, and then McBride was being shown to a suite on the second floor. Apparently, according to the bellhop who had accompanied him in the elevator, there had been an exodus from the hotel the previous evening when the cyclone had closed in. The plywood over the window was banging, and together with a loud permanent roar of the cyclone, speaking had to be at a shout. The bell hop shouted, "Don't sit by the window, Sir. Some debris might pierce the timber." He indicated an upholstered sofa against the opposite wall. "You can watch the TV from here. In the bedroom the bed is against the inside wall. You'll be safe in bed." He was clearly trying to soothe him, except McBride wasn't even slightly worried. This building looked as if it was made with reinforced concrete. No worries. The bellhop added as he pocketed the tip, that the restaurant would be open all day until ten that evening, the minibar was fully stocked, and new supplies could be obtained by dialing housekeeping.

The bellhop vanished out of the door, and McBride went into the bedroom, looked on the dresser, where the bedroom instruction book was, flicked through it, found a city plan in it. Then he took out the address Billy had given him, read it and put the address back in his pocket. Next, he walked back into the sitting room, sat in the chair against the wall as advised, and studied the map. Eventually he found the street he was looking for, circled it using the biro from the bedside table. He put the plan in his pocket as well. He got up, went to the minibar, fixed himself a stiff gin and tonic.

Sitting back in the chair he used the remote to turn the television on, riffed through the programmes until he found the local news channel, and sat back to watch. It was all about the storm. He watched live film showing the dock area, ships smashed like matchwood, small boats halfway up the bluff from the water, waves reaching the main landmass. Sea water flooding the roads at the back of the promenade.

Eventually, he turned the television off, closed his eyes and dozed off.

***

When McBride woke two hours later, the wind was still roaring, the shutters banging and not much else was happening in his room. He went for a wash in his bathroom, tidied himself up, and went down to the restaurant for early dinner. There were only two other people in the room. He sat up at the bar, ate there while watching television again on the news channel. A man dressed in a sou'wester was in the city center telling the camera that the winds would abate later this evening and that by morning the cyclone would have passed and be dying out over the land further south.

He pushed his empty plate to one side, ordered a pint of beer. The two diners, pretty women, at least one of them was, came up to the bar and sat on adjacent stools. The one who sat next to McBride said *hello* in a friendly way. They ordered glasses of wine, and looked up at the television. The man in the sou'wester was back saying the same things again. It was a new take, because this time he had a drunk in the background making rude gestures. The cameraman moved to exclude the drunk.

"The television programme's boring because there's nothing new happening." He looked at the pretty girl on the next stool, and smiled.

She smiled back, showing perfect white teeth. "I know, it was the same before we even sat down for our meal."

McBride took a liking to the girl. "Hi, I'm John. What's your name?"

"Holly."

"Where are you from?"

"Here, Darwin. We didn't want to stay in the public community center. Some awful people there. And some good ones, of course. But here you can pretend you're on holiday. The room rates are real good, too. This storm has really hit the tourist business."

Chapter 26

McBride turned to Holly. "Where is the community center, close by?"

"Just down the street a little way," she frowned and then added, "why do you want to know?"

"I'm looking for a guy. I've got an address, but I've not been round to it yet. I just flew in this morning from Perth, and this damned cyclone got in the way."

"You must have come in on the last plane today. They put it on TV, a camera shot of the plane. How it nearly crashed then tried again, successfully, as you know."

McBride smiled slightly, not even showing his teeth. "I was quite pleased about that."

"So you must be a cop. Chasing a criminal, I mean."

"I didn't say the guy was a criminal. He hasn't been tried yet. But he has been charged, and skipped his bail. I'm not a cop. I think the cops might never catch him themselves, so I'm going to turn him in, that's the idea."

Holly flicked her fingers at the barman, held up her glass. He refilled it, the girl pointed at her friend and he refilled her glass too. Holly looked at McBride, her eyebrows raised. He shook his head. "Not at the moment," he said.

"Why? Are we moving in on the criminal? If so, I'm ready to go." She wasn't even slurring her words. This girl could take her drink.

There was a huge crash and a gust of air as the boarding over the window was ripped from its moorings, and caught the glass as it spiraled away, shards of glass glistening in the air. The wind tore at the curtains, the table linen, cutlery and everything swept across the room, and McBride ducked, pulling Holly's head down.

Her muffled voice floated up from below the bar: "You certainly know how to impress a girl." McBride pulled her up to her feet.

"Come on, we're getting out of here."

The barman said, "All guests out of here now, go to your rooms please, the bar is closed." He added, "And the restaurant, too." He vaulted over the bar counter, and held the door to the corridor open. "Quickly, now."

Once they were in the corridor, with the bar door behind them closed, the sound of the storm was diminished. Holly said, "It's the end of the cyclone, they always end with a sting in the tail. By morning the wind will be nearly gone. You'll see."

McBride said, "Come to my room if you like, I've got a suite, we can use the sitting room. I'm not trying to seduce you girls." Holly's friend said that she was going to bed for one, she'd had too much to drink already. They were at McBride's suite already, on the same floor as the restaurant. He put his card in the door slot, stood back to let Holly in.

"This is seriously posh," she said, looking round, then going from the sitting room through the door into the bedroom. She went into the bathroom. "Won't be a jiffy, I'll repair the make-up," she said.

"Want a drink?" McBride shouted.

"Please."

He opened the minibar, took a white wine shot bottle and glass out, and took them through, put them on the coffee table, sat down on the sofa, and zapped the television. A forecaster stood in front of a map of Darwin. He was explaining that the tail end of the cyclone was passing through the city currently.

Holly came through the adjoining door as the forecaster was saying that, allowing her to comment.

"I told you so."

"He also said that everyone will be free to leave the community center about seven o'clock tomorrow morning. I want to be there then, looking for a six foot tall old man with a beard."

"I'll show you the way."

"Means we must be awake early. If you want to have a sleep in the bed, you can. I had a long sleep earlier today, so I'll read a book and maybe nap here on the sofa."

She sat down beside him, and drank her wine. "You are a spoilsport, sending me to bed by myself." She watched the television for a moment, then turned to him. "You aren't a homosexual, are you?"

"God forbid, of course not. But bedding you when you've had a lot to drink is the next thing to rape. That is not my scene."

She stood up and bent down to kiss him on the mouth. "You are a nice man. Don't forget to take me with you tomorrow morning."

McBride read his book for another couple of hours, then the book fell on to the floor as he dozed, then slept soundly. Old habits woke him at half past five, as he woke he knew that there was something he must do very soon. Memory flooded back. He must go to the community center, see if Harold Fox was there. He went through to the bedroom realizing that there was no wind noise. The silence was unnerving after all this time. He bent over and shook Holly's shoulder. She had taken off her blouse and jeans, she was lying akimbo on top of the bedclothes. He could see her vaguely in the light from the sitting room. She woke instantly, put her arms round his neck. "Come to bed," she said.

"No time, we have to get down to the center, see if my man is there. Get dressed." She put her feet on the floor and yawned. McBride meanwhile opened his suitcase, pulled on a fresh shirt, a pair of jeans. He dug out a pair of deck shoes. These were boating shoes, canvas uppers with rubber soles, with a deep pattern that stopped people slipping on wooden yacht decks. A light form of trainers. He took off his socks, and he was ready for wading. He anticipated there would be a lot of that when they got into the streets.

Holly eyed him. "Oh, we're dressing scruffy are we? I'll just pop along to my room and change. I'll tell my friend, Emma, where I'm going while I'm there. I'll meet you in the foyer, in five minutes, okay?"

McBride went down by the stairs, and emerged at the back of the lobby. Sun flooded into the area, the boarding over the glass doors had already been taken down. A man with a squeegee floor cleaner was sweeping the water out of the doors, leaving the floor tiles bright and clean. McBride went across to the desk. "I'll stay another night, John McBride, in the suite on the second floor."

"Yes, Sir," said the clerk, making adjustments on his computer. "Same rate as last night."

The elevator doors opened as he turned to watch Holly run out of the elevator and grab hold of his hand. She, too, was dressed in jeans and in addition a wooly sweater. They walked hand in hand out onto the main street. There was a lot of debris on the side walk and they walked with care.

Holly pointed across the street. About fifty yards on the right a large building stood, above the windows, in embossed letters the words *Darwin Community Hall*.

"I see it," said McBride. Uniformed staff were unbolting the doors and flinging them open. Almost immediately a crowd flooded out into the street, many of them carrying carrier bags and blankets, talking and shouting at each other, they turned both ways, up and down the street, mostly on the side across from Holly and McBride. They paused to watch, looking for a tall old man with a short beard. A short beard because he wouldn't have had time to grow a bushy one. It was very difficult to judge by size, because the white Australians have over the generations grown into a well-built race, and the average height of most males is six feet. The aborigines were slightly smaller but McBride was filtering out anyone not white. Holly was sensibly keeping quiet, as she didn't know the guy they were seeking. She did tell McBride that the address he had shown her on the piece of paper he kept in his pocket was further up the main street, so they moved past the hall so that they could concentrate only on the people going in that direction. McBride was surprised that the hall held so many, but Holly explained that it had been built to hold rock concerts amongst other big events like international boxing matches.

"It's no good, Fox could have already gone and we didn't spot him. Or he could be waiting in the hall for someone to meet him. Or he might never have been there."

"Well, let's go to his house then," said Holly. "It's only about a mile away."

"Okay."

It was actually further away than Holly had estimated. As they got nearer to the port area, the water was standing quite deep in depressions. They had to wade through, as McBride had guessed they might. It didn't matter for him, in his canvas shoes, but Holly was wearing stout brogues that looked as if they might be spoiled by the water. She stopped and took them off, tying the laces together, and slinging the pair round her neck. She looked as if she was enjoying the outing.

They got to the street where allegedly Harold Fox lived. It was a fairly new, though down-market housing development. In England they would call it *affordable housing.* The houses were actually bungalows, all individual houses but packed so tightly together they might well have been a terrace.

"What was the number on the paper? Can you remember?"

"Number 176." She examined the numbers on the gates. The even numbers are on this side, and odd numbers on the other. Come on."

McBride didn't move. "The cyclone must have blown my brain away. Hang on, this is not the way to do it. If Fox sees me coming along the road and he's in his house, he won't answer the door, and I'll be spotted by him. He's going to vanish. What we need to do is hire a car and park up close by. If you're with me that will look as if we're just stopped to have a talk or something. If Fox leaves the house, I'll break in while you watch in case he comes back too soon. But if he comes back when I'm inside, then when he returns I'll immobilize him. Tie him up, maybe. I'll need some rope with me. Then I leave him there phone my contact in Sydney Police and tell him where Fox is, and he can get the local police here to carry out the arrest. Job done."

"Okay. Come on then. Hire a car."

"Better still, you go and hire a car. I'll hide across the road, by that bush there," he pointed.

"I don't have enough money to hire a car. At least, I don't think so. How much do you think it will be?"

She was not worldly wise, thought McBride. But why shouldn't she have been through her short life never having the need to hire a car?

"We only need a small one, say a Ford Fiesta, or a Toyota Yaris. Something similar. Do you have a driving license with you? One with no penalties on it?"

"What do you think I am? Of course I've got a license and I don't have penalties." She took a swipe at him, laughing.

McBride fished out his wallet, pulled dollar notes from it. "It shouldn't cost more than $100 a day. But you might have to leave an extra deposit, so I'll give you two hundred." And maybe I'm misjudging you, I might not see you again, but there you go. I'm taking a chance. Or rating you as okay. We'll see.

"How long do I rent it for?"

"Just a day. If you go back to the hotel, there's a booth in the foyer where they do car rentals. Hertz, I think. When you've got the car come back here, and park near to number 176, and blow your horn. Only once, though. I'll come out as quick as I can."

"Okay," she said, "I'll be back as soon as I can." She stuffed the notes in her coat pocket, turned and walked rapidly back up the street." Maybe, thought McBride, it was goodbye. He would see. He looked across at the large bush, more a tree. It had been incorporated in the development. Perhaps the council had dictated that the tree, bush, whatever it was, could not be felled. He could see, now he looked more closely, that the road had taken a bend to miss the item of vegetation. He walked across, stepped behind it. He couldn't see the street at all. He moved slightly so that he had a view that included the door of 176. Each bungalow was about four feet from the next. A small path to get round to the back. There was a hard-standing for a single car in front of the window, and a path up to the front door. The hard-standing was flooded, how deep was hard to judge, unless you lived there. But the water was below the top of the step under the front door. So it was unlikely there was water in the house, unless the water had been higher during the storm. McBride was glad, anyway, that it was not his property.

Chapter 27

Time passed. McBride leant against the tree trunk. There was nowhere to sit unless he came out of his hiding place. He was tired now, not having slept for long the previous night. He should have gone to bed. But if he had got in with Holly, what sleep would he have got then?

He was jerked out of his reverie when he saw a small car slow down and turn onto the hard-standing of the bungalow. A Volkswagen, it looked like, a nondescript grey. He saw the exhaust pipe cease to belch noxious gases. No sound then. The driver door opened very slowly, and a large man climbed out. He was six foot tall or more, and he had a close cropped sparse beard. It was a like his head, coarse hair but a mixture of patches of brown and the beard hair was sparse. He had only seen Harold Fox once, and without the facial hair, when he was kidnapping McBride in Melbourne. On the other hand, he seemed a lot younger. You wouldn't class this man as in his early seventies. Definitely not. Maybe his son?

The man paused when he was at the front door of the bungalow, digging in his trouser pocket for his key. When he had it in his hand, he stood on the step above the waterline, pulled his wellington boots off, stepped into the house in his socks.

Meanwhile, McBride had been crossing the road, and ended up only feet away. The man looked across at him, standing with his hand on the door. McBride didn't stop walked through the tiny garden, made to climb on to the bungalow doorstep. Fox pushed the door to close it, but McBride pushed it violently inwards. He heard a bang as Fox missed his footing and fell backwards on to the hallway. McBride followed in behind the door, bent down and pulled Fox to his feet, then took a hefty swing and punched Fox in the jaw. Fox went backwards reeling, and clutching at the walls, pulling brass ornaments that went clattering to the floor. He ended up at the end wall, arms akimbo. McBride pushed the front door violently closed behind him.

McBride said, "This the living room?" pointing to the door on the left, grabbing Fox by his arm. Fox nodded. McBride dragged him through the door. The room was small, a bay window to the front of the building, another window at the back looking into a small garden, and beyond that yet another row of bungalows in the next street. The day was dull but no longer windy. Splashes of rain hit the window and water trickled down the panes. He happened to glance up towards the ceiling, saw a large damp patch, the plaster sagging ominously.

McBride said to Fox, "You've lost a few tiles off the roof, looks like." Fox looked, didn't comment.

McBride pulled a dining chair from the table, signaled Fox to sit down. He noticed that the man had a robust belt round his waist. He pointed and said, "Take your belt off, give it to me." Fox did nothing just gazed back at McBride, who grabbed at the belt, unbuckled it violently, and with one pull, removed it from his trousers. He got hold of Fox's arms, pulled them behind the high back of the chair, bent down holding tightly to Fox's arms while he wrapped the belt round the man's wrists, and then through the spells, fastened the buckle. He tested whether Fox could get free. It seemed unlikely.

McBride went round the chair, sat on the edge of the table, bent down close to Fox. "Now we talk, and I get to beat you up a bit. For various reasons. Let's start. Firstly, you kidnapped me and dumped me on an island. You must remember drugging me, and abandoning me. Do you know it took me nearly a week to get back on the Aussie mainland. I lost a few pounds in weight, though. That was good."

The man tied to the chair looked up with a puzzled look on his face. "You must be mixing me up for someone else. First off, my name isn't Fox. There was a guy lived here called Harold Fox, until a couple of weeks ago. I took over the tenancy. The landlord would tell you where he is, I reckon. I can give you the telephone number of Egbert Bakkar, that is the name of the landlord. He rehoused Fox in a house in Fannie Bay. Fox apparently thought this house was a bit below his standards. Still, it suits me. Well, it did do until you came bursting in and beating me up. If you just open that drawer in the dresser, the top one, there's my passport, in the name of Joseph Prince. Just get it and then release me."

McBride, now embarrassed, scratched his head and said, "It was the beard and this address that put me off. I did think you looked a bit young, though." While he talked, he was untying the guy from the chair. Joe Prince sat massaging his wrists while McBride went over to the dresser, pulled open the top drawer, spotted the UK passport straight away, pulled it out, opened it to see the name and photograph.

"Yeah, you are Joe Prince, right enough. And British, too. My sincere apologies. I got carried away there. You wouldn't believe what Harold Fox has been up to."

Joe now stood up. "I suppose I might have acted the same way in your shoes. I'll get Bakkar's phone number, and you can use my phone." McBride thought that Joe had been exceptionally understanding about his cock-up. If the positions were reversed, McBride knew that he would have been very annoyed.

A car horn blared once from the street outside. McBride said, "That will be my lift. Let me go talk to her a minute, while you get the phone number." He dashed outside, waded to the white Fiesta which had pulled up to the kerb-side. Holly stuck her head out of the driver's window, puckered her lips and gave him a big kiss.

McBride said, "We got the wrong house. He's moved. I'm just going back to make a phone call to find the address. It's in Fannie Bay. You know it?"

"Course I know it. Everybody does, it's seriously upmarket."

McBride gave her a kiss, plunged back to the house, sending spray as he went. "Back in a second," he shouted as he ran.

McBride ran back into the house. Joe Prince was still in the living room, standing now, with a piece of paper in his hand. Prince said: "Here's the landlord's telephone number, you can use my landline, like I said."

McBride smiled at him, picked up the handset, dialed. The phone rang for a few seconds, then: "Bakaar".

"Hi, I'm downtown with your tenant, Joe Prince. I came to town, and thought I'd look in on my friend. It seems he's moved to Fannie Bay without telling me. I'm leaving town tonight. Can you give me his new address?"

"Your friend said not to give anyone the new address. I suppose he didn't expect you to turn up, though. He's on Crescent Street, number twenty. Don't say I told you, or he'll kill me. Okay?"

"That's a promise. Thanks a lot."

He said goodbye to Joe, and went out again to the car. He climbed in.

"It's number twenty, Crescent Street. Think you'll be able to find it?"

Holly smiled at him as he strapped himself into the front passenger seat. "With your eagle eyes peeled you should be a good helper."

She turned the car in a three-pointer in the waterlogged road, and slowly made off back to the main street. Then she did a left to go past their hotel.

"Would you just stop outside the hotel, and I'll get my case. Then I can go straight to the airport later?"

Holly shrugged. "Sure." They pulled up in the unloading area off the street.

McBride went to the reception area. "I'm going to have to leave town. The room I booked for tonight. Could I cancel?"

"Sure, Sir. Shall I bring your suitcase down from your room?"

"That would be great. Thank you." He peeled a ten dollar note off a wad in his pocket and laid it on the counter.

Chapter 28

In a short time they arrived at Fannie Bay, marked by a sign on the side of the road. Underneath the name of the area, the sign said *Home of Fannie Bay Gaol*.

McBride said, "Home of a gaol? Who would advertise that?"

"It's well known tourist museum now, used to be a gaol until the late seventies. Oh, and it's an art gallery, too. Mostly aboriginal art, I think."

"Pity we don't have time to go see it," said McBride.

"Hey, I'll tell you another story about the place. It has a famous stuffed sea crocodile called Sweetheart. The name was nothing to do with its temperament, it's named after the sea creek that was his home. The croc is huge, over five meters long. He didn't attack people, but he hated outboard motors, and would attack those. It meant he often tipped the occupants of the boats into the water. Experts said the noise of the motors sounded to him like a rival male croc. Someone suggested moving Sweetheart to a zoo.

They tranquilized the crocodile, and while they were hauling him to the bank, he got dragged underwater after he got tangled with a tree branch and was

drowned. Then they decided to have him stuffed and displayed in the museum. Sad tale really, and a sad end for Sweetheart."

McBride said, "Good story, though. Also I've just spotted Crescent Street, it's the next turn on the left. Pull in beside the house before number twenty."

The street was tastefully landscaped with the houses set in large lawns and no boundary fences between the houses, which McBride bet would cause a lot of friction in future years. There wasn't a person or vehicle in sight. Each house had a double garage, and presumably the tenants put their cars away if they weren't using them. Eerie.

Holly had stopped the car. "Leave your engine running," said McBride, "then if things get a bit nasty, drive off. Not that I expect that to happen." He opened the car door, got out smartly and walked with purpose up the drive of number twenty.

There was no sign of Fox, or anyone else looking from a window of the house. Maybe there was nobody at home. When he arrived at the front door and saw the large peephole sat in the middle at head height, he had a gut feeling that there was trouble shaping up. These feelings, when he got them, mostly turned out to be accurate harbingers. And he paid attention to them. Therefore he pushed the bell and immediately stepped to one side with his back against the wall adjacent to the door. And waited. A man from the house opposite opened his garage door, and pushed a lawn mower on to the grass. Nothing else moved. Holly was watching through the windscreen of the hired Fiesta.

And then McBride heard the sound of the door next to him slowly opening. What happened next wasn't slow. Harold Fox, preceded by a double barreled shotgun in his hands ran out of the door, and simultaneously the gun was fired. A huge blast and a hail of pellets blasted down the drive. If McBride had been in the doorway, he would have been dead or dying. As it was, he watched Fox run past, and then ran behind him. So far it seemed that Fox was unaware of McBride, concentrating on the Ford car and making for it fast.

Holly reacted straight away and started the car moving towards him, mounting the sidewalk and then across the lawn, picking up speed, giving McBride as onlooker the impression that she was intent on running Fox down. McBride could see that Fox would fire at the car with his remaining shell up the barrel. Already he had the gun up to fire. Suddenly, Holly was no longer visible behind the windscreen, but the car didn't stop. Fox pulled the trigger as he lost his nerve. McBride winced. The car windscreen turned into a white sheet, before the glass dropped in a myriad sparkling diamonds, leaving the open interior of the cab. As the car hit Fox in the knees, and he slumped forward on to the bonnet head down, Holly bobbed up behind the driving wheel, pulling the car wheel so that the car pulled back towards the road.

Ignoring Harold Fox, McBride pulled open the car door, reached over and switched the ignition off. He kissed Holly and asked, "Are you all right, Holly, are you hit?"

"I don't think so, just covered in this blasted glass. Look out, the man's moving."

McBride reached over, grabbed the gun and tossed it a few yards away on the grass. He hefted Fox by the back of his jacket onto the lawn. He lay on his back, eyes closed, and McBride grabbed his arm, felt for a pulse. It was beating very well for a man his age. He slapped his face very hard, shouted, "On your feet, Fox. I want to talk to you!"

He looked up. "I've been run down by this car. I think I've got a broken leg. I need to go to hospital."

"You deserve everything you got. Going round shooting people with a shot gun."

CHAPTER 29

Holly was out of the car, shaking herself as though performing a modern dance. Glass beads flashed in the sun as they scattered from her clothes. As McBride approached her she stopped her prancing, began taking her outer clothes off shaking each item with outstretched arms. More sparkling beads dropping to the ground.

She said, "Unless I get stripped off completely I'll never get rid of this beastly broken glass. And what are the rental people going to say?"

"They are going to say that's what insurance is for, and sue Harold Fox for damages. And once they get here they might say, *what the hell are you doing naked?*"

Suddenly Holly pointed and screamed. "He's running away!"

McBride swiveled round. Sure enough, Fox was on his feet and running, or rather, limping away down the street. By now the area was rather busy with onlookers standing outside their houses, drawn out by the sound of gunfire.

McBride started running after him, shouting. "Stop that man he's a criminal!"

One or two of the men standing in their gardens started to drift unenthusiastically down to the street, the bigger guys going with more haste. Before McBride could catch up with Fox, one of the neighbors had grabbed him by the shoulders, and immediately Fox fell to the floor again. The guy who had grabbed him let go and looked around embarrassed.

McBride caught up with them. "Thanks," he said. "Help me get him on his feet." They reached down and each got hold of an arm, pulled Fox on his feet. They kept hold of him, not because they were worried that he might get away, but that he might fall down again. Together McBride and the neighbor walked Fox back to Holly's car.

"Holly, use your cell phone to get the police. Dial the emergency number, three zeros ask for police, tell them we've caught a man that is wanted for murder, name of Harold Fox, and tell them where we are 20 Crescent Street, Fannie Bay."

Already Holly had the cell phone to her ear waiting to answer. Then she started speaking.

McBride was relieved. If they could keep hold of Fox for about five minutes, his fate was sealed.

The big neighbor reached in his pocket, and pulled out a .38 pistol. That's what it looked like to McBride. Well that solved the problem of how to control Fox. He took his hand away from Fox, relaxed and looked at Holly. She was staring in horror at something behind McBride.

McBride turned to see what had happened. The neighbor was pointing the pistol at him, not at Fox. McBride raised his arms. The man said: "We're leaving, Fox and me. If you let me have the keys of the car, I won't shoot you, or the lady."

Holly reached in the car and tossed them to the man, who caught them without moving his gun. He said to Fox, "Harry, get your shotgun. It's over there on the lawn."

He watched him while he stooped with effort and picked up the gun. Then he limped over to the car and sat in the back. The man with the keys climbed into the driving seat. They looked out through the broken windscreen. He started the car and went rapidly down the road.

Holly was bent over laughing. McBride said, "What the hell do you find funny about Fox getting away?"

"That's what's funny. The car's got no petrol in it. I was supposed to fill it, but we never got chance."

The car was about three doors further down the road, now doing kangaroo hops as the petrol ran short. The car free-wheeled to a stop.

They heard the sirens of approaching police cars. The two men in the rental were getting out of the vehicle and running, or in the case of Fox hobbling back to Fox's house. It looked as if they were going to hole up there.

The first police car stopped beside them. "You made a call to us?" The cop in the passenger seat leaned out, pointing at Holly.

"Yes it was me. Look they tried to drive off in my car, but it ran out of petrol. Looks like they are running into Fox's house. They've got a shotgun and a pistol."

The cop climbed out, un-holstering his gun. "If they're holing up, then we'll soon have them, dead or alive. Worst thing they could have done." He leant back into the car, spoke to the driver, who unhooked the radio, and spoke into it urgently for a minute or two. Then he got out of the car, spoke to the other cop.

"I've ordered backup. They've given an ETA of ten minutes. Six more guys, including two firearms men. And we'll have a stack of Kevlar vests as well."

McBride walked over to the cop standing on the lawn. "If I can help you, let me in the house. I'm ex SAS Regiment, and used to this sort of thing. Remember the guys who stormed the Iranian Embassy in London? They were SAS men." What he didn't mention was that he was not one of the men taking part. It took place the year McBride was born.

The cop eyed McBride with more respect. "We're not supposed to put civilians in danger, so my first thought is no way. But I suppose if you gave me a written statement that it was your wish to do this, I suppose I could turn a blind eye. I could say that you are mad to do it, mate."

McBride just shrugged. They stood around waiting for the reinforcements to arrive. There was no movement to be seen at Fox's house.

Chapter 30

Holly sat on the grass, McBride chatted to the cop, going over the Harry Fox saga, which he was not up to speed about. He hadn't had time to look at the details, being dispatched urgently to Fannie Bay.

A police van came down the road, lights flashing but the siren turned off. It pulled in behind the police car, and police in combat dress including bulletproof vests piled out of the sliding doors. McBride was impressed. The first responders dug out loudspeakers from the police cars, and everybody looked ready to go.

Before anything happened the cop told the crew leader what McBride wanted to do. The crew leader looked at McBride, weighing him up.

"Let me think about letting you into the property. It will depend on how it pans out." He turned to the first responder. "We'll try and talk the guys out first off." He walked over along the road to a position opposite the house. He had his Kevlar vest on, the speaker in his right hand, lifting it to his mouth, pressing the switch by closing his hand. A faint feedback whistle could be heard. Then he spoke:

"Mr. Fox. Please come out without your gun. If you come on out, we will have a talk together. If we have to come in for you, it will be straight to jail."

The answer came back almost at once. An upstairs window hinged back and a double barreled shotgun poked out. It was pointed high, as if to shoot down the seagulls. It exploded and McBride could see the cloud of pellets against the sky. He remembered that Fox had emptied both barrels when he was outside. He had more ammunition indoors. At least a box of fifty, McBride reckoned. Less three at least. Enough to keep the police around here for a day or two. After that they would make a mass assault on the house. And, as a result, if anyone was killed questions might go up as far as Canberra. Police would get sacked. It made it more likely that McBride would get his own way.

McBride walked over to the crew leader.

"I've a feeling this may go wrong."

"What are you talking about?"

"Let's go over to the van and talk it over."

The crew leader looked at McBride for a minute or more, presumably making up his mind whether he would lose face or not. Then he said, "Come on, then." They walked together over to the people carrier. The crew leader took the driver's seat and McBride climbed into the front seat next to him.

"First off," said McBride, "I'm not telling you how to do your job, you've probably been doing this nearly all your life, with total success.

"My interest is that I'm after seeing that Harold Fox stands trial, too. He's a pedophile who's killed at least two children, and some older people. He's a nasty piece of work. I'm an artist now, but for a big chunk of my life I was in the British army, in the SAS. We did the hard jobs, including getting people out of buildings. Like we did the Iranian Embassy hostage job in London. Not the army, but the SAS. I think I could get into that house over there," he pointed, "with you diverting their attention, and I could get Fox, bring him out. Hopefully with all of us still alive. What I'm trying to tell you is that I've got experience doing that."

"I'd need to check that, cover my back, before I let you."

"No problem, my CO is still serving, he would vouch for me."

"Give me a telephone number," said the crew leader. "In the UK, and I'll get headquarters to speak with him."

McBride fumbled in his pocket, pulled out wallet, flipped through. He brought out a card, SAS symbol on one side, address and phone numbers on the other. He scribbled the CO's name on the card. "Go and phone. I need the card back."

The crew leader said, "This will maybe take an hour to sort out at headquarters plus phoning and so on. Best meet me back here in an hour."

"Okay, I want to see the museum. When you come back have a floor plan of number twenty with you. A couple of stun grenades would be invaluable, but maybe that's too much to ask. I could do also a loan of a pistol, maybe .38 or even .44."

He watched the cop drive off, then turned to where Holly was still sitting on the lawn chewing a blade of grass. "How about an hour at the museum? Then I might have a job to do. It's only a short walk, come on."

"Yes, we should, and get the rental replaced. You could phone them while we walk to the museum."

"Then we'd better walk past the car first. I've left the paperwork in the glove box." So they got the documentation, and it was McBride who made the phone call using Holly's phone. The rental company agreed to meet them in Crescent Street, in an hour or so, with a replacement car.

The sun was hot and the sky clear of cloud, and it was a pleasant five minute walk to the museum. McBride was pleased when he found out that it was free admission. For him, the aboriginal art was a revelation. It was brightly coloured with a strangely alien look to the twenty-first century, mind. It wasn't necessarily the style that McBride ever imagined he would change to, but on the other hand, he wouldn't mind a piece or two hanging on his walls at home. Holly grew a bit restless while McBride was pondering over the art, and he found her looking at Sweetheart the unfortunate crocodile. When you stood close, it really was gigantic. What were his last thoughts as it drowned by the hand of these pesky humans? Had he been thinking that attacking outboard motors was the wrong strategy?

McBride thought that, even as a gaol, it was primitive. In its time it had been a mixed gaol, men, women and children. The kids were housed in cells which had wire netting walls, so that staff could check on them. Prisoners were there for fairly minor offenses, right the way through to murder. Two prisoners were hanged in the nineteen fifties for the murder of a cab driver. The gallows used are still there. The prison was still in use up to the end of the nineteen seventies. They requested a donation for visiting and McBride gave without hesitating.

They walked back to Fox's house hand in hand, Holly softly singing a song McBride didn't recognize. He was busy looking at the bay, and mentally composing paintings.

As they approached the house, a lot had changed. There were more police vehicles, mostly parked up on the lawns, leaving tyre ruts criss crossing the grass. Striped security tape was strung all over the perimeter of the scene, tied to tree trunks, car door handles, even parts of number twenty, the house in question. There were a lot more cops there, too.

McBride looked for the crew captain. He was back there, the only cop in a yellow jacket, presumably denoting authority. Or perhaps not. Still, he was the guy McBride had promised to report back to. He lifted the tape. Several cops were looking at him as he crossed towards the leader. Someone spoke to him, gestured towards McBride. The crew leader spun round, recognized him and beckoned.

McBride said to Holly, "You stay here, so that you can exchange the hire car. I shouldn't be gone more than an hour, then I will have to set off for the airport."

He turned and went under the tapes and across to the crew leader.

The crew leader waited for him, then said: "I've got permission to let you in. You've got to sign a waiver though, to protect us in case things go wrong."

"Things?"

"Things like you get killed. Nothing to do with us, in that case."

"Understood. Did you get a plan of the house?"

"Yep. Come into the car and look at it, no point in those in the house getting any ideas, or it will be more difficult for you if they expect you."

He led the way into the people carrier, and he handed a couple of A4 sheets to McBride, who said, "A bit tiny. Difficult to read."

"All I could get at short notice."

McBride spent several minutes studying them, then said to the cop, "So I think I'll go on to the garage roof which is flat, and I assume asphalt covered on timber beams. And planks I hope. From there I will climb into the bathroom here, either break the glass, or if I'm lucky the window could be open. They often are. From there I've got to be careful. I assume Fox is in the front bay windowed bedroom, can you confirm?"

"Yes, he's used his shotgun to fire at us a couple of times while you were away. From that room. But we haven't spotted his pal. Course he might have dodged out earlier. But you should expect to meet him in there."

McBride folded his map and put it into his pocket. He got out of the car, and asked the cop to radio the man behind the house to expect him.

"Two men at the back now. I'll make them aware and to expect you within seconds."

Chapter 31

"Did you manage to get me a firearm?" asked McBride.

"I'm not allowed to even lend you one. Dead against police rules. Because I don't have to account for tear gas grenades, I've brought you one, and a pair of goggles for you. You should cover your mouth with a handkerchief. It helps, but don't blame me if you get a reaction, should you use it. Good luck."

McBride got out of the police vehicle, walked round the back of the house taking a wide route so the occupants were unlikely to see him. He approached from the wooded back of the house, and met suddenly with the two cops that were on lookout.

One of the cops said, "Sneaking up like that nearly got you shot. What do you want?"

The other one said, "You're the nut that's going in. We were talking about you."

"What I'm going to do is get on the garage roof, and from there through the bathroom window."

"The top window's open, so that would be possible."

"Okay. Have there been any signs of life on this side of the house?"

"Well, they use the bathroom as you might expect. And the kitchen, but that's all."

"Okay, so if one of you will give me a leg up onto the garage, I'll get started."

One of the cops led the way to the side of the house along the garage. Apart from the bathroom window, there were no windows on this side of the house. McBride followed the cop, who judged when he was opposite the bathroom window, even though you couldn't see it from here. The cop clenched his hands together in front of him for McBride to step up.

McBride effortlessly stepped up and grasped the concrete slabs of the parapet on the wall, and dragged his body up, let his body fall on the concrete slabs and jacked his legs over. He waved down to the cop in thanks, then ran bent over to the window. He put his hand through the open top window, got his shoulder wedged through and managed to get his fingers round the main window handle. He wrenched the handle upwards, and the main window swung out. McBride stooped and stepped through the main window, and put one foot on the WC top, and from there to the floor. He reclosed the main window and looked around the bathroom. It was about ten feet along each side, with both bath and separate walk-in shower. The door out was closed, and no sound came from the other side of the door. McBride put his ear against the wood to check. Alongside the door was a cupboard; the door the full height of the wall. McBride guessed it was an airing cupboard, but opened the door which was held closed by a ball catch into the jamb. As he expected it was an airing cupboard with a cupola, copper and radiating warmth. Alongside it, shelving with towels and clothes stacked. There was a space alongside the shelving at least two feet wide. He wondered why it was built this way, and saw a step ladder against the wall at the back. But it was not folded up but stood up in the space. He glanced up to see what might be above. A trapdoor, presumably into the loft.

He closed the cupboard, put his ear to the main door again. Sounds of feet in the corridor. Slowly he pulled the cupboard door towards him, climbed in and pulled the cupboard door closed with a hook on the inside of the door. The ball catch clicked quietly. He heard the main door open and footsteps going across the bathroom floor. Towards the toilet pan, he bet. Sure enough the footsteps stopped, he could hear a zipper, then the sound of water running. Urine, he bet. One of the men having a piss. He breathed out slowly. Undiscovered unless the guy opened the cupboard for a new towel. No, the footsteps receded the door opened and he could hear no further sounds. The dirty sod didn't even wash his hands. He heard the door close, and then, before he had time to leave the cupboard, McBride heard a sound up in the ceiling. He glanced up, and in the daylight illuminating the cupboard through the gaps in the door, saw the hatch in the ceiling hinge back, and in the darker square, a face peered down. Bright eyes, small round face, dusky skin, dark curly hair. An animal, was McBride's first thought. As the small black eyes opened wide, and the mouth opened in fear, the hatch closed with a bang.

The attic would need investigation, McBride knew, but first, it was the men with the firearms that needed priority. It was no good knowing what was in the attic when you are dead. He opened the cupboard door, made his way cautiously to the bathroom door, listened and hearing nothing slowly opened the bathroom door.

He could see into the short passage about four feet long, and then a cross passage. He knew from the floor plan of the upper floor that turning left would lead to the front bedroom where Fox had been seen looking out. He was likely sitting and looking out now, with his shotgun in his hand, or close by. Turning in the other direction would lead to the staircase, and now, as he listened he could hear somebody climbing the stairs. McBride went into the cross passage quickly, closing the bathroom door behind him. He pressed his body to the right side of the passage, preparing to attack.

The man emerged, holding a cup of tea in his right hand, nothing in the other. McBride lashed out at his head, hitting him hard, and knocking him across the corridor, the teacup splashing liquid in all directions, cup and saucer crashing into the wall with some noise before pieces of china fell to the carpet. The man had fallen head first on the floor, struggling to rise. McBride kicked his head. The man moaned. McBride leaned down, pulled the man by his shirt into the bathroom passageway.

A shout from the front of the building. "Jimmy, you fallen over?" It was Fox, thought McBride, and went down the corridor towards the front bedroom, the teargas grenade now in his right hand. As he pushed open the bedroom door which had been ajar, McBride saw Fox getting up from an upright wooden chair, his shotgun held with the butt on the floor.

A shotgun is not an easy weapon to handle in an enclosed space. The gun which is allowed to be purchased with a license is only a maximum of two barrel, with a maximum load of two cartridges. It is illegal in Australia to own a pump action shotgun.

The legal gun's use is designed for open spaces, pointed to the sky, aiming at birds, or clays zooming across one's field of vision. To try and wield the gun with its relatively immense size in a confined room is difficult. Re-arming the gun after a maximum of two shots, is also difficult. On the other hand, once loaded and aimed, one does not need precision as the spreading pellets will hit everything in sight. Because there are multiple pellets, the propellant's power is spread amongst them, so at long range they are of limited use.

McBride took in the scene, lobbed the tear gas grenade at Fox, then pulled the door abruptly closed.

Immediately, McBride heard the man called Harry scuffling around, getting to his feet perhaps. McBride thought what a fool he was, trying to tackle two men at once and failing not once, but twice. From the coughing and gasping noises coming from the front bedroom, he guessed the most urgent place to be was the corridor outside the bathroom. He doubled back at speed, round the corner and saw Jimmy clambering groggily erect, clutching the wall, and with the other hand trying to extract the pistol from his pocket.

McBride pulled the man away from the wall, and he collapsed back on the floor. He got hold of the man's right hand round the wrist, and squeezed hard, at the same time pulling at the pistol. He yanked suddenly and the gun came loose and ended up in McBride's grasp. He stepped back and said to the man on the floor, "Get up now, or I'll shoot you through the head." The man got up immediately and stood in front of McBride looking down at his feet. He pushed the man through the door into the bathroom, got a large hand towel off the rail, roughly turned him so that his hands were behind his back, and began to use the towel as a rope, binding his hands together so tightly that the knot could not be reached and undone. Then taking another towel, he tied the man to the rail.

The gagging noise still emanated from the bedroom as McBride reached the closed door. Closed was good. He wasn't fit enough to open the door, unless he was trying to get out of the window. No problem about that; the entire Northern Territory police force, it seemed were downstairs in the garden. McBride quickly opened the door, holding the captured pistol in the other hand. *Damn it, he hadn't checked that the thing was loaded. Fingers crossed.*

The scene in the bedroom was of Fox leaning over the chair near the window, head down, and coughing, red-faced, getting close as he could to the open window to take gulps of air when the coughing allowed. He was an old man, and McBride felt momentarily sorry to see him in such a state, until he remembered that the man was a pedophile. Already the pungent fumes were fading, and McBride did not even take out the goggles for his eyes. He looked round for the shotgun, and found it lying on the floor by the window. He picked it up and held it ready to shoot. The handgun went into his trouser pocket.

McBride was under pressure because he was determined to catch a plane to Melbourne that night. He decided to leave the other guy still tied up in the bathroom. With some difficulty he got Fox down the stairs, and then opening the front door which still had the key in the lock, he pushed Fox out holding the shotgun on him, until a cop had grabbed him. Only then did he break the gun, and take out the cartridges, both of them. Fox had reloaded the gun since he had last fired. He showed determination, if nothing else.

One of the cops caught hold of Fox and shouted for oxygen. While two men attended to Fox, McBride explained to the crew leader that the other man was tied up in the bathroom. The shotgun he handed to the cop, together with the two live cartridges from his hand. One or two cops came by shaking his hand and McBride grinned at them. He told the crew leader he must be on his way to Melbourne shortly, but he was going back inside to check the attic.

He didn't think there was any danger from that direction, he told the crew leader. So he was going back inside, but somebody else could get the fellow tied up to the radiator, who was unarmed, so no problem. One of the armed policemen said he would come in with him, and escort the criminal back outside. Then he would stand outside while McBride explored the attic.

When McBride got upstairs again and went into the cupboard, he left the door open, and climbed the stepladder. He reached the top step and extended his arm and pushed upwards. The trapdoor pushed open with a bit of effort. McBride was surprised, and at the same time he heard, a rumbling noise as articles placed on the trapdoor fell off. Somebody was trying to block the entrance. A very young mind was behind the pathetic attempt. What McBride had seen was not an animal, but a small child. How could his mind be tricked into seeing an animal? Because, McBride realized, he hadn't dared to see a child, because that would mean Fox was up to his old tricks.

While he stood there on the top of the steps it occurred that one of two alternatives went through his mind. Either Fox was keeping the girl prisoner, or that the child had escaped and was hiding. Both of these alternatives sickened McBride.

He came down the ladder, sat on the bottom rung. Kept quiet for ten minutes, but nothing happened. While he was sitting there, McBride was thinking about the problem. Assuming the child had been molested by Fox, and why else was the girl in Fox's house, then she would automatically fear all male adults, including McBride himself. He couldn't chase her out of hiding, the girl would be terrified. Whatever could he do? He guessed the signal that brought her out of the loft. The second closing of the bathroom door. The only way she would possibly come to an adult, would be to a woman. It could work. If she asked Holly to come in by herself, and stayed outside, guarding the house, it could be the start of confidence building to a child who had nearly lost everything.

McBride got up quietly and took off his shoes. He held them in one hand and crept out of the cupboard, went out of the bathroom leaving the door open, put on his shoes in the corridor, went down the stairs and out of the main door of the house.

The police activity was winding down. He could see the crew chief, still in his yellow jacket, waving some of the cars off the lawn. The police van that had arrived first, was waiting to go. He could see Fox in the back, together with his friend and four uniformed police in with them. As he watched the vehicle joined the short queue in the road, all vehicles pointed out of the Crescent.

McBride walked over to the crew captain. "Can you spare time for a short discussion?"

"Sure," he said, "but I thought you were in a hurry to catch a plane out?"

"I was, but I think I've missed it, and the job isn't finished. Can I explain?"

"Yes, come and sit in my car." They moved across to the big saloon with badges on the doors, but no blue lights. A captain's car, McBride thought. The captain got in the driver's seat, leaned across and opened the front passenger door.

"Get in, and tell me what the problem is."

"There's a young girl in the attic. I saw her, and I saw the terror in her eyes. You know why?"

"Tell me what you think."

"She has been assaulted by Fox. What other reason is she there, hiding in the attic. And she is frightened of me, and all men, I suspect." He looked at the captain closely. "I want to try something else. To send Holly, that's the girl I came with, to go in there alone and try to sweetheart the girl down, and get her confidence to come out with her. Surely you don't object to that. If the police are all men, I guess to go barging in there something nasty may happen."

"We do have police women. I could get a pair of them up here in what, half an hour?"

"Do they speak the language?"

"What language? What are you on about?"

"I saw the girl. She's aboriginal, I'm sure."

"Does your girl speak aboriginal?"

McBride shrugged. "I'll find out now." He opened the door and climbed out of the car. Holly was sitting on the grass still, content in the hot sun, eyes closed. The new hire car was close by, a different colour this time, fire engine red.

"Holly?"

"Yes. John? You have missed the plane, I guess?"

"Maybe. It's not important. I can't get the girl who is in the attic to come to the hatch. She's scared of men, not surprisingly. I'm hoping you will go up there without me, and maybe coax her out. But the girl is aboriginal. Do you speak a bit of the language?"

"You sure are a lucky man. If it's the local language, then yes. I did a course at college, all about the locals. And yes, I can get by. But if she isn't from this state, then it will be like chalk and cheese. We'll both be talking different tongues. There's about two hundred or more languages they could speak, It's the dialects that are unintelligible to others not from the vicinity."

"Then can I co-opt you? To bring her down?"

"Yes. I'll go up there. If she's been up there for long don't you think she might be hungry?"

"Yes, very. But not thirsty, I reckon. I think she comes down to the bathroom when no-one is around, to use the loo and get a drink of water. I hope she gets washed too, but until you see her, you won't know."

"Shouldn't we pop down the road, get some food, and maybe milk as well?"

"Good idea. I'll just tell the captain, ask him to hang around a while longer."

McBride stood up, went back to the captain, who was standing outside his car now, looking over to McBride. As McBride approached him, the captain said, "What's the verdict? Is Holly going to do the job?"

"Yes. Well, she speaks the lingo, so that makes her good to go. We're just going to get some milk and food. We reckon the little girl might have been up there a while. We'll be back in about five, ten minutes."

Chapter 32

Holly said she would drive, got into the hire car, and they were away.

McBride said, "Do you know a shop round here?"

"Yes, I'm surprised you didn't see it. Right across from the museum. Looks like a mom and pop set up. Sells everything, General stores. Open all hours I'm hoping. We'll soon see."

She was drawing up outside the store as she spoke. Lights were on, and the door was open. They walked in, grabbed a wire basket from the pile by the door. She walked confidently round the tiny store. McBride followed, a little perplexed.

"Have you been here before? You seem to know where everything is."

"Most of these convenience stores, they work to a common plan. For example the milk is on the way out. It's a last minute thing. You know, *oh, and I need some milk.* And the papers are near the checkout. For the guys who come in on a morning for the news, and haven't time to walk round the store." She grabbed some cheese, a packet already sliced. She went back round to where the checkout was, on a couple of shelves she pulled ready-made sandwiches, in cardboard packs, with cellophane windows, showing the filling.

"I think that will do," she said, and heaved the basket on to the shelf for unpacking. Then she added a packet of mixed sweets as an afterthought. The old lady at the checkout had everything into a brown paper bag in no time.

They came out blinking into the sunlight, and Holly stashed the bag on the floor of the car in the back foot well. In five minutes they were back at Fox's house.

She left the car on the roadside, got out of the car, waving at the police captain, and came across the lawn carrying the bag of food.

"I'm good to go," she called to the captain. McBride walked along with her until they reached the house door.

"You go to the top of the stairs, take a right, and then a left, there's a door at the end of a short passage. The bathroom door is at the end. Open it, wash your hands in the basin, then slam the door, but stay inside. Sit on the chair that's near the door. And wait. It might be several minutes before she comes out. She's got to climb down the steps. When she sees you she will be scared. Smile, and speak to her in aborigine, offer her a drink of milk, and take it from there. I'll wait here at the door all the time you're in there."

Holly gave him a smile. "Don't worry. I'm not." And she started up the stairs, with the food bag tucked under one arm.

McBride sat down on the doorstep, looking at the sunny view. There were no houses across the road and he could see through the trees to the sea. The captain came over, said, "I'm going now. Lots of policing still to be done. I'm leaving one policeman with you. He's in the car down on the road. Once you're finished in the house, he's to lock up and take the keys with him down to the police station. Is that okay with you?"

McBride stood up, shook his hand. "Thanks for all you have done." Then he sat down again, watched the captain get into his car and drive off. He put on his sunglasses, thinking about the act showing he was a pom, and smiled. He leant against the door jamb, and closed his eyes. He wondered how long Holly would be before she came down with the child. He drifted off to sleep.

Chapter 33

Holly sat in the chair in the bathroom. There was no sound except the annoying drip of the bath tap. She found herself counting the seconds between each drip. Fifty-seven, on average. It varied by no more than four seconds. God, it was driving her mad. Her eyes closed.

It was a scuffling noise that woke her. For a second or two she didn't know where she was. Then her memory came flooding back. She turned her head to the cupboard on her left. The sounds were coming from there.

Holly started counting again in her mind. She stopped herself. She would start to go mad with this obsession. As she watched, the cupboard door swung open. The girl couldn't have been more than five years old. He clothes were dirty. She wore a dress, socks but no shoes.

She saw Holly and shrieked. Holly smiled and held out the carton of milk.

The child swung the cupboard door shut behind her. There was a total silence. Holly was sure she was standing just behind the door.

Holly was patient. She no longer counted seconds or even minutes. But it seemed a long time before the cupboard door pushed open again, and a tiny face peered out.

Holly smiled at her again, and held out the milk carton, which had remained in her hand for the past few minutes.

For a few seconds, or even a few minutes, neither of them moved. And then the child edged forward. Holly said in aborigine "come and drink." The child smiled back now, and held out her hand. Holly gave her the carton which she had already opened. The child took the carton, eagerly began to drink.

The child handed back the carton. At that moment, Holly heard a rattle from inside the cupboard. Astounded, she watched the door slowly open. Another child stepped out. Another aboriginal child. In a dirty dress. The first girl went over to her, and took her hand. Holly held out the milk carton again. The first child took it, and handed it to her companion. She spoke one or two words. Holly understood. They spoke the only aborigine language Holly knew. Her heart lifted. All that study at college had not been in vain.

Holly held up the grocery bag. "You want to eat?" she said in aborigine.

She held the packet of sandwiches out. Held it up for their inspection. The first girl took hold of it. She struggled with packaging. Holly gently took it back, and opened the package, gave each of the girls half of the contents. They ate greedily, and then shared the rest of the milk carton content.

Holly decided it was time to swap names. "Me Holly," she said, and pronounced her name again. The girls each parroted her name. "Olly," they said, repeating it several times.

Holly said, in aborigine: "Your names?"

The first girl, the one Holly had known longest, and who had the curliest hair said "Kirra," and patted her chest. She repeated it several times. The other girl didn't need asking.

"Bindi, Bindi Bindi."

Holly stood up slowly, so as not to alarm them, and spoke in their language: "Next we wash, hands and faces, and next we will go out."

They dashed over to the washbasin, ran the taps and doused their faces and hands, using the soap, having learned that, but not to use the plug. Holly joined them, and performed her ablutions, too. They stood back to watch.

Holly said, "Now we go out, to home." She watched their faces closely, to see their reaction to the words in aborigine. Both girls looked at her and both smiled. They each held hands with her. Holly opened the bathroom door, and there were tears in her eyes.

McBride heard the footsteps coming down from the first floor. It had woken him, and he stood up, and moved out into the garden. He didn't want to alarm the child.

He moved away and Holly appeared in the doorway. She had two children with her, one holding each hand. They stood blinking in the sunlight. Two dirty clothed aboriginal children, aged about five years old.

Two children. McBride was shocked. Never in a million years would he have thought that there was more than one child hidden upstairs. Holly was waving to him now, and he waved back. She was taking the children to the hire car, putting them in the back seats, and getting into the driving seat. She waved again as she drove off. She mimed holding a telephone to her ear.

McBride wandered over to the policeman sitting in his car by the road edge. He had the window fully wound down and was reading a paperback. He looked up at McBride as he approached.

"Hey, so you got two more people out of the house. Amazing. Are you done, now? Shall I go and lock up the house?"

"I'm sure the girl will report back to you. I think she will have gone to have a word with Aborigine Council in Darwin. I can usually guess her mind."

The policeman started up his car, and McBride watched until the car had turned at the top of the road and vanished. Everybody was leaving him.

He took his cell phone out. He didn't know Holly's phone number. He put the phone back in his pocket. Just then it began to ring, and he answered.

"Hey it's Holly here. I've just brought the kids back to my apartment. I'm sorry I had to go, but the kids saw you and were really frightened. I thought they might turn round and hide in the house. I didn't want to go through all that again."

"No, of course not." He still felt hurt.

"I'm getting in touch with the Aborigine Council in Darwin now, and perhaps they might know about the kids being missing, and if you've missed tonight's plane, and I can tell you, you have, why not come back into Darwin, stay the night at the hotel you stayed at before, and I'll see you tonight. I can get a baby sitter, or I might have got the kids placed with their mums." All this in one gabble without stopping until she was breathless.

"It's a possibility. Why don't I go get something to eat in Fannie Bay, and then you can phone me back?"

"Will do, honey. Two hours, tops, bye." And she was gone again.

Chapter 34

McBride was sitting in an upmarket teashop in Fannie Bay. He had eaten a cream tea, consisting of many teacakes and sweet cakes, and drank a couple of cups of tea. After all, he had not eaten all day until now. They had raced out of the hotel without breakfast in an attempt to waylay Fox after the cyclone had abated, and then chased him in Fannie Bay. Then assisted the police in capturing Fox and his neighbor from the house they were holed up in. And last of all they had got the aborigine kids out of the attic.

It had been a tiring day without having time to eat until now. All McBride was waiting for was a telephone call. He looked at his watch, two hours up. And as he looked at his watch, his phone rang. It was Holly.

"Amazing timing, I just look at my watch, two hours. And the phone rings."

"You know I wouldn't let you down. I've just spoken with the aboriginal community people, and yes, they have a couple of children apparently kidnapped when they were out playing. The lady in charge is rounding up the parents, and bringing them down to my apartment. They should be down within a few minutes.

If you want to hail a cab and come down here, you'll be able to witness the reunion." She gave him her address, and he wrote it down. Then he was out of the tearoom, and right across the road was a cab rank. Within two minutes of her phone call he was on the road back into Darwin.

The apartment block that Holly lived in was quite posh. He paid off the cab, and pressed the bell for Holly's flat. She answered and buzzed the main door open.

McBride bounced up the stairs to the second floor, Holly's door was ajar, so McBride knocked and walked in. There was a great deal of noisy voices, and childish laughter.

Holly spotted him coming in, and introduced the mum and dad of the kids who were twin sisters. They solemnly shook hands with each other. And then McBride was introduced to Bindi and Kirra, who also shook hands with him. Kirra spoke in aboriginal, and Holly translated. "She says thank you for finding us."

The aboriginal family had been brought to Holly's apartment by the community minibus, and it was waiting outside. Holly and McBride accompanied

the family downstairs to the street, and stood on the pavement to wave them off when they were in the bus. As the bus disappeared round the corner, McBride swept Holly off her feet.

"You're one in a million," he said "saving two kids' lives."

"You found them," she said. "Come on, I'm so hungry you wouldn't believe. Let me drive you to the hotel, and we'll rent the biggest suite in the place, and eat a banquet. Afterwards, we'll, well wait and see what happens."

Holly drove them both to the hotel they had stayed in last night. The same desk clerk was on duty. "My, you're back again so soon. Tell me you want a couple of rooms for tonight."

McBride smiled. "No, we need one suite tonight with a king bed. Can you do that?" While they were at the desk, they booked a table for two in the restaurant.

They went up to the suite which was on the second floor, and the bell boy came up with them, carrying their luggage. He went into the room first, piled the cases on the luggage rack, showed them the features of the suite, and left with a hefty tip from McBride. Holly spent what seemed to McBride as a long time in the bathroom, and came back out, showered and dressed only in a hotel white toweling robe, as McBride quickly found out. They stretched out on the bed over the top of the bedclothes.

"Excuse me for asking," said McBride, "but are you a virgin?"

"Certainly not, but the problem with most men is that they are only after one thing: wham bang, thank you Ma'am!"

"That must be just the Darwin men."

"All men. In my experience."

"But until you met me you thought I was homosexual, remember."

"Okay. Except you. Are you married or something?"

McBride smiled, looked up at her. She was sitting looking down at him. "I was, but the army intervened. It ruins lots of marriages. You are away a lot of the time, abroad mostly. If your wife comes with you, she is left in scruffy married quarters, or she stays at home, and sees you at infrequent intervals. It's not a recipe

for a happy marriage. We parted amicably, though. And we didn't have any children.

"I heard that she married again, and has a family, two children. We swap cards at Christmas."

She sat back, taking it in. "I wouldn't have guessed," she said. "Would you marry again?"

McBride laughed. "Are you proposing to me?"

"No, I don't really know you. But you seem a nice guy."

He rolled over on his elbows, looking at her. "Thank you very much. I think I'm too old to marry again. The army made me restless. I'm still always on the move. This year Australia, all last year touring the United States. That was because Ian Smith, my agent, insisted in the nicest possible way that it would increase my fame, and his commission, though." He smiled at her. He reached out, and she moved to kiss him.

***

A lot later Holly sat up in bed, and said, "Thank you, you are something different. A man that makes a woman feel very, very, happy. But now I'm extremely hungry. I haven't eaten all day long. No breakfast, lunch or dinner. We are going to go down and eat lots of food. Now!"

She got up and vanished into the bathroom. McBride lay back in the bed with a feeling of contentment. The bathroom door burst open and Holly rushed across the room dressed only in her bra and pants, opening her case throwing clothes on the bed.

"If you don't get up and get ready, I am going to dinner without you. Go on, get into the bathroom!"

He ambled off with his clothes. He got into the shower, soaped himself down and ran the water cold, which invigorated him. He dried himself briskly, used the hairdryer which was on the unit containing the wash basins, smiling at himself in the mirror. Nothing like sex to perk you up, he thought. And to give you an appetite.

The Maître'd sat them in a table in the window overlooking the main street, where they could look down at the people shopping. The daylight was fading and the street lights were on, the shop windows brightly lit. There were plenty of people about, perhaps because of the cyclone having kept them indoors. McBride was looking at the menu.

"Let's really push the boat out, have every expensive dish here, eat really well. We deserve it for two reasons, well three reasons. He counted on his fingers. One, we captured a really nasty pedophile. Two, we saved two children from an attic. If the house had just been locked up, they could have starved in there. And three, and most importantly, well…" he looked at Holly and giggled. She reached across the table and batted him with her menu.

"You go on like that, and you'll be on short rations".

McBride looked down at the menu again. "How about oysters to start? Followed by steak tartare? Not too filling."

"It's something filling I need after starving since yesterday. I'm going to have a bowl of oxtail soup with lots of crusty bread. Then sirloin steak with chips, and mushrooms."

"We will both have our own choices, I declare. Oh, and a bottle of Sancerre. Does that suit, Madam?"

"Well, one bottle to be going on with."

The wine was served ahead of the food, and they toasted each other with a smile on both of their faces.

At the end of the meal, Holly said, "Gosh, I never told the police that I'd found the children's parents, and reunited them. God, the police will still be messing around with the case."

McBride said, "I don't think it works that way. They'll probably contact you about it tomorrow. Don't they have your phone number, or at least your name?"

"I don't know, I can't remember. They have your name though. Can you phone them and tell them."

"Maybe. Did you have the parent's name?"

"Well, no. But I have the name of the Aboriginal Committee lady." She dug in her handbag, pulled out a card handed it to McBride. He pulled out his phone. Got the number of the Darwin police from directory enquiries. Told the police lady who answered about the Fannie Bay affair, the capture of two men, one being Harold Fox.

He asked if he could speak to the crew leader, if he was still there. There was a long pause on the phone, then a click, and a guy said, "Don Gates here."

McBride recognized the voice. "Hey Don, sorry to bother you, but you remember the two aboriginal children we pulled out of Fox's house this afternoon. Well, Holly here just reunited them with their parents, through the Aboriginal Committee here in Darwin. The committee contact was," he pulled the card across the table towards him, read aloud, "Mrs Daniella Watts. There's a phone number." He read it out.

Don said, "Yes, I know the lady. I've made a note, and I'll contact her in the morning and get the kids' names. Thanks a lot. Take care." And the phone went off.

The next morning they were up early for McBride to catch his plane to Melbourne. He should have gone the previous day, but didn't finish the Fox business in time.

They walked side by side to the car, and Holly got into the driving seat, McBride in the passenger seat, fiddled with his phone: "Jack Hopkins, please. We got Fox, yesterday. Brought him out of his house, he's in police custody, in Darwin. I'm getting a plane to Melbourne this morning. By the way, we found two aboriginal children, five years old, hiding in Fox's attic. Up to his old tricks again. Make a note. Have it brought up at any trial Fox has. I don't want him doing a short prison term. He needs to be locked up for the rest of his life. I'm relying on you, Jack."

"Don't worry, I will. Thank God you are going back to Melbourne. I've been thinking that your agent was going to have a heart attack. He's ballistic about you not being painting in there and earning him a crust."

"It's more than a crust he takes from me. Do me a favor. Get hold of him, and tell the guy that I start painting today, four or even five paintings a day, until we've got the right number."

Hopkins said, "I look forward to seeing you when I come over to the exhibition. Good luck."

Holly pulled the car into the short term car park at the airport. McBride glanced over at her, and saw tears rolling down her cheeks.

"What's the matter? You're crying." He was concerned.

"It's because you're leaving me. Just as soon as I think I know you."

"I've got to work, and I suppose you have. You could come to Melbourne with me if you think you can get a job. But don't forget I have to work, so I won't be with you all the time. Let me get my tickets and we'll have a coffee together and discuss this." He pulled out his unused handkerchief and dabbed her cheeks dry.

They walked into the terminal hand in hand. McBride went to the ticketing counter and Holly looked at newspapers in the kiosk close by.

McBride joined Holly at the kiosk. He waved the ticket envelope, and put it away in his pocket.

"Shall we go for a coffee?" said McBride.

"Yes, let's," she said. "I've decided not to come to Melbourne with you today. But that doesn't mean I won't come later on. Give me your phone number and I'll give you mine. We'll keep in touch, I hope."

"Certainly will. If you do come, you can stay with me, I shall get an apartment in a week or so, I can't stand longer than that in a hotel."

They walked arm in arm to the coffee shop, and later she walked with him to the gate, and waved as he walked through the security check.

About The Author

Hi, I'm David Chilcott, and I've been writing now for about five years. I'm a mechanical engineer by training, but I became a serial entrepreneur. I sold my last company a few years ago. For the last twenty years I've been a professional artist, painting exclusively in watercolour, so it's no surprise that is what McBride, my fictional hero does. I live in Yorkshire.

WWW.DAVIDCHILCOTTAUTHOR.COM

Printed in Poland
by Amazon Fulfillment
Poland Sp. z o.o., Wrocław